Into the Ruins

Spring 2020
Issue 15

COPYRIGHT

Published February 2020 by Figuration Press
Portland, Oregon

Into the Ruins is a project and publication of Figuration Press,
a small publication house focused on alternate visions of the future
and alternate ways of understanding the world,
particularly in ecological contexts.

intotheruins.com

figurationpress.com

ISBN 13: 978-1-950213-02-3

Editor's Note:
A busy winter, an unexpected delay in publication,
a skipped season, and changes coming.

Comments and feedback always welcome at editor@intotheruins.com
Comments for authors will be forwarded.

Issue 15
Spring 2020

TABLE OF CONTENTS

PREAMBLE

STORIES

CODA

PREAMBLE

A Moment of Reckoning

by Joel Caris

I ALWAYS ENJOY THE TURN OF THE CALENDAR. The tick from December to January is a reset for me, the opening wide of a new world of possibility and the promise of a day of quiet reflection with which to kick off those new possibilities. I actually, in some ways, wish this was different; I would like for the winter solstice to be my mark of annual renewal, my internal clock set the same as our planetary one. Old habits are hard to break, though, and I did not grow up celebrating the cycles of the sun. I grew up celebrating the religious marks on the calendar: Christmas and New Year's Eve and New Year's Day. And so it is that first day of January, the turn to a new calendar, that most grabs my imagination and orients me to a new annual phase of growth, that yearly opportunity to conceive of ways to make myself anew.

On that first day of the new year, I typically set pencil to paper to record a series of resolutions for the coming months. Some of them I achieve. Others fade into neglect and forgetfulness as the year carries on. But there is a promise to them in the year's early days that inspires me, sparking hope that I may yet make myself into the person I hope to be. I understand that there is a certain danger in this kind of thinking: a provisional living that can foster constant unhappiness; a risk of failing to live well the life that exists today rather than what might exist tomorrow; a consistent uneasiness and dissatisfaction too easily preyed upon by the more predatory elements of our culture. I have succumbed to all those dangers at times in the past. But now I see my resolutions as less dangerous than they may have once been. Granted, I can approach them with a zeal bordering on obsession at times—my wife could tell you stories—but for the most part I see them as a chance to think, reflect, and reset: to seek each year to become a better person while being careful not to condemn the person I already am.

One of my common failures during this process, though, is forgetting that the *continuance* of good and useful habits is a valid resolution, as well. I always want to layer on new goals and objectives, new habits I want to establish or quicker travel down a path I already am walking. I see nothing wrong with that, of course, except when it risks derailing the good work I already am accomplishing and want to continue. After all, there are only so many hours in the day and one has only so much expendable energy; we all must contend with our limits and what we can accomplish within them. One of the more self-defeating habits, to my mind, is derailing an already-existing good habit in the hopes of creating a new one.

My wife Kate reminded me of this as we sat in a coffee shop on New Year's Day talking over some of our resolutions. One of hers was to continue to successfully feed us. It may sound at first blush like a modest goal but it takes honest effort when one considers the way we eat. Not that we don't go out to eat, but we eat the majority of our meals at home, cooked from scratch and based on as many local and seasonal ingredients as possible. I don't mean that as a boast; that just is the way we like to eat. And due to my past work on small-scale farms growing vegetables and raising animals, I feel a particular connection to such a way of eating. Kate and I like being connected to our food, knowing where much of it comes from and who grew or raised it—often being friends with them, in fact—and knowing that in our eating we are supporting our local economy and community.

But it *is* a way of eating that takes some planning and foresight. That means we always have stock bags in the freezer for veggie scraps and bones and that we often pull out the fireless cooker on weekends to make a batch of stock for the week; that means remembering to soak beans, make crusts in advance, and regularly have a few meals planned out; it means boxes of potatoes and onions and garlic and shallot and grains and dried pasta under the couch, particularly in the winter; it means pulling the meat out of the freezer in advance, planning for roasted chickens and pot roasts on weekends to help fill lunches during the work week, and canning tomato sauce and jam and freezing diced peppers and celery and jars of homemade pesto in the summer and fall; and it means making sure we are available when the winter farmers markets take place so we can supplement with fresh greens and whatever storage crops we don't already have in the fridge or under the couch.

It's not the easiest way to eat. But it's not the hardest way either, especially once you get used to it. It's definitely, to our minds, the *best* way to eat. I don't mean that in a moralizing way, though I like to think the way we eat makes the world a tiny bit better and hopefully helps keep some of the remaining small farmers in business; mostly, I just mean that it's the tastiest way for us to eat and what makes us feel the best now that we have grown used to it as a diet. The planning and foresight is key, though—just like line drying our laundry, growing some of our own food, putting up preserves, or meditating daily. And it's not something I want to do for a year and then quit. It's how I want to live my life. Which means that it's fair game to serve as a resolution every year, to not just build new habits but to continue the ones I (or Kate) have already fought for.

That said, I am a sucker for ambition, even if I have a tendency to lose the thread over the course of the year. And so I strive and reach, writing down some of my fondest wishes, sometimes being overly specific in those wishes, and aiming for a transformation each new year. It's an old story for me by now, but yet I somehow find something new in it every twelve months. In particular, that has been true of recent years.

I wrote about this before, back in the Spring 2019 issue of this magazine. In recent years, I have had more success with my resolutions and with the forming of better habits in general. I suspect that partly has come due to a more settled and satisfied life thanks to my marriage. Probably it also comes from age, from the slow process of finding my footing, from experience and the sometimes painful process of building self-awareness and self-knowledge. They have led to small revelations, these better habits, and a growing confidence that I can accomplish long-sought goals and that I am capable of being more disciplined than I once thought.

That confidence received a particular boost recently. A few months back, I started several major new practices. That isn't what I normally do; generally, by the time fall rolls around and the calendar starts flicking toward the holidays, I pick up my reading and perhaps start casting my mind toward the coming new year and its possibilities, but it is rare for me to tackle any serious new habits requiring focus and effort late in the year. However, something fell right this year and, as summer transitioned into fall, I began meditating and conducting a daily banishing ritual, focused on tackling a series of practices I had long considered—even attempted a few times—but never committed myself to.

I won't go on at length about my experiences, but I will note that they took for me, and I am practicing them both to this day. The results have been considerable and, to be honest, I'm surprised at how well I have stayed on track with the effort. Granted, I would not say the practices are hard per se, but the commitment to practicing daily and making time for them is significant. There are days when I do not want to take the time, when I do not want to expend the modest effort, or when I am upset or scattered or disjointed, and the thought of focus, attention, and honest effort is dispiriting. Of course, those are the times I perhaps most need to engage in my practices, as they have a tendency to calm, refocus, and recenter my mind, orienting me to the better possibilities of the day yet ahead.

They also help to lift me above my daily joys and travails into a wider perspective of my life. As meditation has moved me toward a greater stability and peace, it helps me better understand the long-term desires I have for this life of mine. And as it has also given me a boost of confidence in my ability to tackle long-sought goals, a sense of where I might best put my energy and activity has started to become clear to me—and in the process, changed my perspective on what my day to day life should perhaps entail.

As already noted, though, it is not always an option simply to layer in new activities. This became abundantly clear to me last summer as I simultaneously tried to maintain my regular day job and my marriage while also taking on a significant contract job, working to put out an issue of *Into the Ruins*, finishing a story on deadline for a contest, and planning for a camping trip at near the same time. A bit too much of life converged on me all at once and, while I did not regret any of those activities, I regretted taking them all on in such a short period of time.

The stress and challenges that arose from that stretch of activity, as well as some of the discussions I had with my wife as a result of those, is part of what spurred me to take on meditation and ritual in the early fall. The meditation subsequently brought on a significant amount of introspection and self-evaluation, while also leading to a new flare up of trouble as I worked through some of my internal issues. All of that has lent me new perspectives on my life that still are evolving to this day.

However, as I move into the new year and think about what I want of this life, I have arrived at some reckonings. I also have arrived at a moment in which I feel a strong need to step back and evaluate, to recenter and calm myself, to bring new space into my life so that I can prepare for the next changes I suspect are coming. There are things I yet want to do with this life, some of which I already am working on and others that remain within reach but not yet fully grasped. There are people I am committed to—first and foremost my wife—who deserve a full version of me, rather than a scattered and distant one too consumed with other work and projects to be fully present in our relationship. And there is important work I am doing that I am not willing to give up.

Yet there is only so much time and energy and space, and that's where my reckonings come in. I both need to choose where I am going to focus my energies and to what degree I am going to step back to create an equilibrium from which to launch whatever is to come next in my life.

As I have considered that question over the last few months, a framework for the coming year has started to emerge. It involves giving more time to my own writing, both for stories and essays, and seeing what I may make of that with dedication and perseverance. It involves continuing my meditation and related activities and studies, and seeing where that takes me. It involves being healthier, having a bit more time for thought and reflection, and bringing a greater balance to my life. It means considering acquiring new skills—studying bookkeeping, perhaps—and trying to better understand where I want to go next in this life.

There's more, some of it a bit too personal to elaborate on, but one of the overriding feelings I have is that I need to take a step back, relinquish some responsibilities I have taken on, and reestablish myself in this world—in some ways unchanged and in other ways different. One of the ways I need to take a step back, though, is with the publication of *Into the Ruins*. I have decided to end the magazine after the upcoming sixteenth issue, which will complete four years of publication. It has been a hard decision for me, and one I have considered for awhile. In many ways, I do not want to step away from this magazine. It has been a delightful project, profitable in multiple ways, and the home of a committed community full of people I have really come to appreciate it. I am most of all, in this decision, sad about walking away from that community—from all of you reading this who have been such excellent and dedicated followers, thoughtful and kind in your interactions with me, supportive and enthusiastic about what I have attempted to do with this project, and smart and insightful in your evaluations of this strange world we inhabit. *Into the Ruins* has become something special and unique and particular in these past four years and I have really enjoyed the opportunity to harness the energy of its community of readers and writers and artists in its creation.

I also believe that there is still very much a place in this world for a magazine dedicated to deindustrial science fiction. I wish it could continue to be *Into the Ruins*, but I also see no reason that it can't be something else. If anything, I fear that my own particular worldview and editorial vision has too constricted this space at times, cutting off opportunities for creative offshoots that might take the genre in exciting and diverse directions, into a more complete ecosystem from which to launch genuinely new types of science fiction visions. That is, of course, no knock on the stories that have seen publication in this magazine's pages. I love them and have been continually surprised and gratified by the quality of writing that comes my way; that said, I want also to see what a different editor might bring forth from those voices hosted by this publication and those who have yet to find *Into the Ruins*—or even the subgenre of deindustrial science fiction. I suspect there is much yet to be discovered in such tales of the future, and as the world around us quickly changes, I want to see what new voices—not just authorial, but editorial—can make of its future given the new raw materials of our time.

I hope that happens. I want this project to continue on in a different form, and I want the community that has formed here to find itself a new outlet. I know this community won't go away; much of it is borrowed (thank you John Michael Greer) and interacts together not just here but in other venues. But I love to see its regular expression in the realm of fiction as well as in those other venues. And so I put forth that mantle in the hopes that someone will take it up. Know that if someone does, I will support them and encourage the *Into the Ruins* audience to do the same.

All that said, I come to this decision, to my future, even to this new year with a strange sense of optimism I did not necessarily have four years ago when I started this project. Partly that is rooted in the changes I see in the world around me. I do not cheer many of those changes, but watching it change so dramatically—that gives me hope. It tells me that dramatic change is possible, and given that I think that necessary for us to make the future better than it may otherwise be, it breathes a bit of life back into my visions of useful adaptation.

Partly I come to that optimism due to the changes in my own life. It is a better one than four years ago, even though it has its challenges and complications. I have changed dramatically, as well, and in those changes I see hope for the kind of future for myself I have long dreamed of.

And partly I come to that optimism due to the experiences of publishing this magazine over the past four years. It is heartening to see the ways that community has formed around this; heartening to see the positive reception and dedicated support; heartening to see so many respond so enthusiastically to a strange creative vision put out into the world these past four years. I thank all of you for your support, your kindness, your commitment. You have made my life better, and hopefully this magazine has made yours a bit better, as well.

This is not the final issue of *Into the Ruins*. That will come in late spring or early summer, with the release of the Summer 2020 issue, and I will no doubt have plenty more to say in that Editor's Introduction as I grapple with the ending of this project. In the meantime, though, I hope all of you come into 2020 with hope and optimism, with a dedication to making this world better, and with visions of a future that, while no doubt sure to be full of challenges, beckons us forth into creative construction, into the making of a world better than the one we find ourselves in today. I cannot thank you enough. I hope you find the stories in this issue as enjoyable as always, and I look forward to a fantastic denouement in the final issue yet to come.

— Portland, Oregon
January 18, 2020

Questions? Comments?

If you have questions about the coming end of *Into the Ruins*, contact Joel Caris by email at joel@intotheruins.com. If you have comments, concerns, or any insights you feel may be helpful, please do the same. All subscribers whose subscriptions extend past the upcoming sixteenth (Summer 2020) issue will be contacted and offered a refund.

All issues of the magazine will remain available for purchase for the foreseeable future. To purchase past issues, please visit intotheruins.com or contact Joel Caris at the above email address.

I believe a quarterly magazine of deindustrial science fiction remains an important and financially viable project. Should someone else start such a magazine to fill the gap left by the end of *Into the Ruins*, I will happily publicize and support it. If you or someone you know is interested in starting such a project, please do not hesitate to contact me at the above email address for thoughts, advice, and support.

Some form of *Into the Ruins* may yet reemerge in the future, perhaps as a one-off anthology or a more sporadic series of publications. Similarly, your friendly editor does not expect to remain quiet for long. While *Into the Ruins*, at least in its current form, may be coming to an end, my own writing will not.

Interested in staying up to date on both accounts? Please visit and follow joelcaris.com to stay apprised of Joel's writing activities and to receive announcements of any future publishing projects. Also visit Figuration Press, the small presss that releases *Into the Ruins*, at figurationpress.com to stay updated on any future projects.

Thank you for all your support of *Into the Ruins* over these years. It means the world to me. I hope you will continue to follow me at joelcaris.com and that you will support any new deindustrial SF publications that arise, of which I'll keep you informed.

10 Billion

A Graphic Novel Based on the Story by John Michael Greer

Available in Early 2020

For more information visit next10billion.com

Into the Ruins is published quarterly by Figuration Press. We publish deindustrial science fiction that explores a future defined by natural limits, energy and resource depletion, industrial decline, climate change, and other consequences stemming from the reckless and shortsighted exploitation of our planet, as well as the ways that humans will adapt, survive, live, die, and thrive within this future.

One year, four issue subscriptions to *Into the Ruins* are $39. You can subscribe by visiting intotheruins.com/subscribe or by mailing a check made out to Figuration Press to:

Figuration Press / 3515 SE Clinton Street / Portland, OR 97202

To submit your work for publication, please visit intotheruins.com/submissions or email submissions@intotheruins.com.

All issues of *Into the Ruins* are printed on paper, first and foremost. Electronic versions will be made available as high quality PDF downloads. Please visit our website for more information. The opinions expressed by the authors do not necessarily reflect the opinions of Figuration Press or *Into the Ruins*. Except those expressed by Joel Caris, since this is a sole proprietorship. That said, all opinions are subject to (and commonly do) change, for despite the Editor's occasional actions suggesting the contrary, it turns out he does not know everything and the world often still surprises him.

EDITOR-IN-CHIEF
JOEL CARIS

DESIGNER
JOEL CARIS

WITH THANKS TO
JOHN MICHAEL GREER
OUR SUBSCRIBERS

SPECIAL THANKS TO
KATE O'NEILL

Contributors

Joel Caris is a writer, gardener and homesteader, past farmer, passionate advocate for local and community food systems, voracious reader, sometimes prone to distraction and too attendant to detail, a little bit crazy, a cynical optimist, and both deeply empathetic toward and frustrated with humanity. He is your friendly local editor and publisher. He lives in Oregon with his amazing wife, who makes both him and his life better each day. His writings and more can be found at joelcaris.com.

Mir Seidel's novel, *The Speed of Clouds* (New Door Books, 2018) explores the boundary between living on Earth and out in space through the mind of a sci-fi fan. She wrote the libretto for an opera about Nikola Tesla, *Violet Fire*, performed in Belgrade (for his 150th birthday), New York, and Philadelphia. She's also written about art and performance for *Art in America*, *The Philadelphia Inquirer* and other publications, and is now working on a YA fantasy. She tries to stave off climate despair by working with a local branch of 350.org. More at miriamseidel.com.

David England is a ponderer, generalist, and student-of-everything who makes his home in a pleasant working-class community along the western shore of Lake Michigan, where he lives with his wife Anne, her amazing artwork, and the cacophony of voices in his head telling him what to write next. His stories have appeared in the anthology *Vintage Worlds*, the online 'zine *Tales to Astound*, as well as the quarterlies *MYTHIC* and *Into the Ruins*.

Jonathan Andreas is a California librarian by day, a cellist by night, and a doctoral student in between. In his efforts to return to the land he has laid claim to the entire San Andreas Fault. He is, after all, eminently faultworthy. To date, no one has recognized his claim. Jonathan can be found at ecodreamer.net.

Dewey Dabbar is the fiction-only pen name of an amateur field naturalist who lives in a small city in the East of England. There he wanders the surviving scraps of wild land and dreams about what once was and might be again.

CHRISTINE STONE lives on the south coast of England with her husband Ian. They enjoy looking after their garden and playing with their grandchildren. Seeing the little ones grow year-on-year inevitably turns Christine's mind towards thoughts of the future and what their lives will hold. Having lived these past three, nearly four, years surrounded by the Brexit Saga, she has found it somewhat cathartic to imagine a time centuries from now when the details of it are all long forgotten. Christine writes emails and constructs spreadsheets for a living. This is the first story she has had published. She hopes you enjoy it.

A graduate of the U.S. Naval Academy, DEVON MARSH served as a naval aviator in the 1990s. He now works as an electronic payments expert with Wells Fargo Bank, occasionally writing and speaking on payments risk management. Devon also writes poetry and fiction, including the novella *How I Know*, and he edited his late father's WWII memoir, *Never A Hero*. Devon's poems have appeared in *Nightingale and Sparrow*, *The Lake*, *Poydras Review*, *The Timberline Review*, *Muddy River Review*, *Penmen Review*, *Loch Raven Review*, and *The Kakalak Anthology of Carolina Poets*. Devon Marsh lives in the piedmont region of North Carolina.

At the age of sixty-five, JEANNE LABONTE is a lifelong resident of northern New Hampshire. Now retired, she has more time for her main interests: writing, drawing, gardening, stitching and publishing personal observations about them, as well as the beauty of the local environment, in her blog New Hampshire Green Leaves, located at jeannemlabonte.com.

W. JACK SAVAGE is a retired broadcaster and educator. He is the author of seven books, including *Imagination: The Art of W. Jack Savage*. To date, more than fifty of Jack's short stories and over seven hundred of his paintings and drawings have been published worldwide. Jack and his wife Kathy live in Monrovia, California. Jack is, as usual, responsible for this issue's cover art. He can be found at wjacksavage.com.

ALISTAIR HERBERT lives in a small house in West Yorkshire with his wife and their two children. He works part time for a local government organisation, writes stories for *Into the Ruins*, and volunteers with Treesponsibility, a decidedly local group planting trees in the Upper Calder Valley. He posts regularly but infrequently at alistairherbert.wordpress.com

LETTERS TO THE EDITOR

Dear Editor,

I write to thank Al Sevcik for his good opinion and to reciprocate it. His story "First Train to Tampa" in Issue 13 of *Into the Ruins* was an unexpected blend of horror, humor, and human obstinacy on both sides of the Luddite line. In one brief account, he packs in a lot: the real risk of entrepreneurship—the virtues of thinking ahead—strategic surveillance—shifts and nuances in local forms of political power—even a little romance. That's a whale of content in a twelve-page package. I expect Mr. Sevcik has a few good novels tucked up his inky sleeves. Hope so, anyway.

Cheers to all and keep on writing!

G. Kay Bishop
Durham, North Carolina

Dear Editor,

I wanted to share a personal story that I hope will bring some peace as we reflect on the inevitable massive societal changes awaiting us shortly. I lived and worked in Chicago, had a good job that I drove to where I wrote software for other companies that produce software. Sort of a snake eating its tail situation and one that seems common in our world. After a time I grew disenchanted with the life I had. I made nothing that lasted, I consumed nothing that mattered and it felt more and more like I was just running down the clock until I died.

So I decided to move. I left the country, sold my house and my car and got rid of most of my stuff. I live in Denmark now. I bike everywhere I need to go. Taxes are high on luxury goods so for the most part you go without. Food is expensive but it's good and you buy what you need as you go. You don't see security cameras on the street or police officers constantly paroling but there isn't any crime to speak of. Sometimes there are robberies but it makes national news when a store owner is as much as pepper-sprayed, much less more seriously hurt. There is less competition because there is less benefit to "winning." Being rich and buying many items is seen as a negative trait, not a positive one.

There is a government program here where people who don't have access to land are given small plots in the city, leased to them at a cheap price. The idea is that it is good for you as a human being to have some connection to the land around you, to work in the dirt from time and time and even build a small home. This has created a population of people deeply passionate about the health and wellness of their country but also who are connected to it. The children grow up not seeing nature as a removed and isolated event, but as part of their lives.

As a cynic I assumed high taxes and restricted access to items would create black markets and make those items more valuable. Instead it seems to have removed them from the minds of people. Bars here don't have beer from around the world, but usually just the local beer and maybe a few bottles of wine. Parents leave their babies outside to sleep in their strollers, believing the cold helps them sleep and is good for them. It's a startling display of trust in each other for an American. This society where luxury is more inaccessible than home has created a society where people seem to be less afraid of each other.

My point with all this isn't to say "everyone move to Denmark." It isn't a perfect country and has its problems. But I think sometimes we look at the coming changes and mourn what we will lose. Make no mistake, we will lose a lot. However at the end of this road is the possibility of a better, more just society that values things of importance. At least that is what brings me some small bit of hope in a sea of bad news.

Mathew D
Odense, Denmark

Dear Editor,

The Fall 2019 issue was superb! I have enjoyed several reads so far. I was especially taken with Clint Spivey's "Scuttle Star Island." It makes me really sad to think about the ultimate attitude towards Americans as expressed in the story although I can certainly see how that attitude is coming about. Regrettably it is also well deserved. But the story was very captivating and I liked its clear portrait of how humans' natural cooperative nature is easily over ridden by our fears. It is fascinating to me that we clearly would not be here today if it were not for our cooperative nature. It is really too bad that we have so little awareness of this important aspect of human nature. The current political climate is a classic example of forgetting the importance of cooperation. It is also true that being prepared and
careful is good back up.

David England's "Multa Ab Uno" was also a fun read and highlights the value of being prepared for the unexpected. The ending was not what I expected. A good reminder that outcomes can depend on small instances of being prepared.

Sincerely ,

Tom Anderson
Bellingham, Washington

Dear Editor,

I love the covers for each issue. The seasonal themes of each painting are a really nice touch and in line with what kind of stories are contained within. The only thing is, when sitting on my bookshelf, there's no way to see these.

I'm not sure if it's feasible, but is there any way to have a small patch of the cover on the spine of each issue? It wouldn't even have to be that big. An inch of the same color sampled from the cover might look really nice on the spine. Once again, not sure if this is too much trouble for what it's worth, or if other subscribers would like this change, but I wanted to put the idea out there. Keep up the great work!

Tim Ferraro
Undisclosed Location

Dear Tim,

A fine idea indeed! One of the limitations I have encountered with *Into the Ruins* is my own modest graphic design capabilities. I like to think I have made up for this with at least a small aplomb by learning Scribus, the open-source program I use to create the magazine's digital file, and by focusing on use of aesthetically-pleasing fonts and a clean and simple layout featuring a certain attention to detail (that, nevertheless, does not suffer its occasional mistake). However, in necessarily being the most design-dependent aspect of the magazine, the cover has at times suffered from my own skill base (or lack thereof). The initial issues did not have their title on the spine, though I was able to correct that by the fourth issue. For similar reasons—my own conservative nature and desire for the finished printed product not to be defective in its appearance—I simpli-

fied the cover design by capturing W. Jack Savage's fantastic art within a black border, precisely because I did not entirely trust my ability to extend it onto the spine without inadvertently extending it onto the back cover.

Time and attention likely could change this standard, much as I did with text on the spine. However, given the reality that *Into the Ruins* will be winding down after the coming sixteenth issue, it is unlikely I'll tackle this project. However, Figuration Press —the publishing house of my own design, which to date has only published *Into the Ruins* but which may yet eventually publish more—will take your recommendation under consideration. Certainly Jack's artwork deserves the best presentation possible!

Thanks as always for your feedback.

Joel Caris, Editor
Portland, Oregon

Dear Editor,

I've been thinking of letters the past few weeks and when the request came to contribute one for the next issue I knew I would want to write a letter. In this age of high speed, electronic, distracted communication, a letter is a respite, an enjoyment, an opportunity for relaxed reading and reflection. Writing a letter requires one slow down. Replying to a letter requires more effort than just clicking "like" or "retweet." Letter writing may just be a way to rekindle thoughtful long distance communication and correspondence when that is often taken for granted because social media and email are so convenient.

Yet what if we were to collapse now and avoid the rush as John Michael Greer has been fond of saying? What if we live now the way our future selves would have liked us to live today? There was a saying, often written as graffiti in the East German punk scene before the Berlin Wall fell: *Stirb nicht im Warteraum der Zukunft.* Don't die in the waiting room of the future. For those of us who are interested in developing alternatives to the surveilled and data mined "communication" platforms of the day—facespook, jitter, et al.—then perhaps it is time bust out the fountain and quill pens or even a Bic and a book of attractive looking stamps, fine paper or scrap paper, and set about breathing some fresh life into long hand, or clickety-clack typed, correspondence.

Will there be volumes of the collected emails of such-and-such a writer in the future? Maybe so. Working in a library I've seen the preservation of history that can occur because the letters of various folks over the past four centuries have been preserved, then printed and bound for others to read or study. People used to save family letters, having big bundles of them in trunks, and these became a source of solace for kids when parents departed for the great beyond, and of later use to family historians and genealogists. The

past few years I've been sending out Hallow'een cards to friends and family. I don't send out Christmas cards because, well, humbug. Yet I want to get in touch with my friends as the holiday season starts, and in my family that really starts October 31st (or the closest full moon to that date for traditionalists). This year I decided I would start the tradition of including a news letter about the goings on and doings of my family. I sent that out and was delighted to get a few letters and phone calls in return. People were very appreciative. It's also a good chance to humble-brag about anything cool you and yours might have done that year. Your mileage may vary of course, but for those who like writing letters, an annual missive to friendly folks near and far is a fun project.

As a kid my family used to go on trips every fall. Around the time I started skateboarding and getting into the punk scene—sixth grade—I would go out and skate and meet the local skaters. Skating was great for instantly connecting, and it's easy to do as a teenager. I'd make friends on these trips and ask for their address. There was one punk kid I met from North Dakota and me and him kept up a correspondence for years. It was always a pleasure to get a letter from him, as he always included clippings from the tabloid *Weekly World News*. You know, the one that used to have Batboy and Roswell on the cover? Sadly, that fine example of news media is no longer in existence. I continued to write letters on through college, but after that email started to dominate my correspondence habits with the opening of a Hotmail account. (I'm not sure if anyone is still sad that is still barely in existence?)

But who doesn't like getting something cool in the mailbox and opening up a letter? This past month I was asked by a friend of mine from the shortwave radio community to contribute to an Amateur Press Association (APA) he is heading up. I'd not heard of these before but an APA is a group of people who produce individual pages or magazines that are sent to a Central Mailer for collation and distribution to all members of the group. My friend is the Central Mailer (CM) and three times a year I will send him eighteen things that he will put into a bundle to redistribute to everyone else in the group in a big fat mail bomb. No, not a real bomb. We're not terrorists. APAs were and are a way for widely distributed groups of people to discuss a common interest together in a single forum without using the Internet. Many of these were founded in the 1930s and later by fans of science fiction, comics, music, cinema and other niche topics as a way to develop writing, design and illustration skills. I'm super excited to be a part of this one. For the one I am joining there is a yearly dues for membership of twenty-five bucks that covers the costs of the mailings for the CM. I plan on contributing CDs of some music I've made and articles I've written to start. This was also the basic

principle behind the mail art scene.

I think it would be cool to see some APA's develop on topics such as Appropriate Technology, Green Wizardry, deindustrial fiction and the like. It's also cool to have the letters section in a quarterly like this one, where we can all bring up topics dear to our heart. It might be awhile before any of us are sending these by carrier pigeon (if you do please let us know) but it's great to have a place to send and read letters.

Long live the letter!

Justin Patrick Moore
Cincinnati, Ohio

Dear Readers,

The following contribution from Jon Andreas was sent not as a letter to the editor, per se, but as a thought experiment rooted in some of the familiar themes of this magazine. I asked Jon if I could publish it in the letters section and he was kind enough to agree. Therefore, please consider the following as a basis for continued consideration as we navigate our way through this tricky world of ours.

Sincerely,

Joel Caris, Editor
Portland, Oregon

THOUGHT EXPERIMENT: THE HINGE

I've been looking for a good approximation of an ecologically healthy human society so that I might sketch the least damaging path from us (here and now) to it, and help our children to walk that path. It's a complex issue, so perhaps I should start with the basics.

Imagine a very small society, a single family of two adults and two children. Place them in a temperate climate next to a medium-size river and surrounded by a deciduous forest interspersed with large open fields and rolling hills. It might be Iowa five thousand years ago. How do the parents raise the children to be happy, healthy, flourishing members of their local bioregion? In simple terms, they must draw their sustenance from the local wildlife and leave their waste behind just like every other life form. But this is not merely a biochemical arrangement. It is also social (the interaction of individuals), economic (the give and take of resources), and juridical (the retribution of those social and economic interactions), among other things, whether or not humans are involved. If a bird enters another's territory and takes what is not his, retribution may soon follow. Other elements are also involved such as linguistic (intra- and interspecies communication), cultural-historical (passing along techniques to the next generation), and aesthetic (what looks right or beautiful), all of which are readily seen in more complex organisms such as crows or dogs. But among the more complex (so-called "higher") intelligences only humans seem capable of recognizing and then willfully ignoring the checks and balances of a local bioregion's ecological limits.

Back to our little family by the river. What the adults teach the children depends on their level of awareness of the fragility and limits of their local bioregion. How many berries can be picked so as to neither upset the already balanced usage of the other berry eaters nor to destroy the productivity of the berry plants themselves? Before more berry bushes are planted, where would they go and what disruption might they cause? The same should be asked about other food items (flora and fauna) and materials used for technological purposes (stones, trees, etc.). Every living thing feeds off of others and disrupts the local scenery to some degree. This cannot and should not be avoided; indeed, it is vital to the miracle of evolution: turning death into life and disruption into creativity. If the adults in our little family believe they are the only intelligent beings in their bioregion or that their intelligence is so superior to any others that they alone are wise (sapient) enough to decide the fates of the berries and the crows and all their other animate and inanimate neighbors, then the ecological complexity of their neighborhood is reduced to a human technicism measured by progress: from the stone age to the computer age and beyond. But if the adults teach the children by word and action that they are immersed in a web of relationships that has been fine-tuned since time immemorial, then every action—eating, defecating, building, playing—will be done with a sense of responsibility and reciprocity. Besides, children are natural animists, attributing sentience to things around them—until adults disabuse them of such silliness.

This is the hinge upon which human history swings. Do we see ourselves as alone in carrying the obligation to develop the world around us, perhaps with the help of those "below" us and with the supernatural guidance of one "above"; or do we humbly take our place in the mix, admitting that we are the newcomers to the scene and have much to learn from the elder species that have preceded us?

We already know how the first choice turns out, just follow the course of Euro-American (so-called "Western") history. Our little family multiplies over the generations with no thought to the impact on the local bioregion. Forests are cut down for lumber, fields are plowed for food, the river is poisoned with waste, and when more is needed, they either move somewhere else or colonize somewhere else, bring the distant goods home, and ship the waste out. In other words, the entire long-standing, fine-tuned and evolving ecological web is destroyed. With enough pavement and landscaping, the place is unrecognizable from its prehuman days. Just

think of the original old-growth forests of the island of Manhattan. Even our prettiest reconstructions of nature—manicured lawns and golf courses, neighborhood parks, etc.—are ecological wastelands with pitifully little biodiversity and only a strand or two of the former, dazzlingly complex web. If humans are the *sine qua non* of the Earth, if everything is here for us, then supposedly all this destruction is offset by our ingenuity as measured by such quality-of-life indicators as A/C, AI, and CRISPR. I am as guilty of technophilia as anyone, but in the second half of my life I've begun to question the cost—not just that of replacing a cellphone or laptop every couple of years, but for those humans disassembling the toxic parts of my castoffs in unregulated countries, for the nonhumans affected by toxic landfills and ocean-"islands" of garbage, and, ultimately, the cost that the entire modern consumer economy's infrastructure wreaks on local, regional, and global webs of ecological interaction. Is my staying cool on a hot day, or having instant access to all my friends 24/7, or living a few more years worth all of that? I can no longer say yes.

But what are our other options? Have we lost the ability to imagine a truly ecological civilization? It all seems so complex, so insurmountable. So let's keep it simple: back to our little family by the river. Food? Readily available. Indigenous peoples around the world have demonstrated that securing food in an ecologically rich environment like this riparian setting takes only a couple of hours each day. Clothing, if and when needed, and many other creative amenities are provided by culling a couple of the weaker members of the passing buffalo herd. Shelter, tools, and fire are provided by fallen trees, coppicing, and cutting a very few carefully selected trees, all of which would have a negligible impact on the long-term society, intelligence, and memory of the nearby forest.

Now let's fast-forward a century or two. Assuming the family grows into a community, how many humans can live in that location and in what way to ensure the continued flourishing of the bioregion's ecological web? Twenty? Two hundred? Two thousand? Certainly not 200,000 or two million! Obviously it depends on a myriad of choices: How big are the villages? How far apart are they? Do people stay there year round or migrate seasonally? Whatever the case, to keep from damaging—and maybe even to enhance —that area's ecological health will mean a limited number of humans, and a human society knowledgeable in reading the signs of health (or lack thereof). That is the core of the education of that society's children. Eventually the human society might become a part of the broader climax community, finding a kind of stability that could last for millennia. This balance —the "Way"—could be codified and reinforced in story, myth, ritual, and religion, for the real society is never just human but includes all of the re-

gion's animate and inanimate "people."

If our original family of four were transplanted into a less hospitable region, say a desert, then the numbers over time would necessarily be fewer and the traditions different. If they moved to a superabundant place, say a rainforest or massive river delta, then it is conceivable that many more thousands of humans could live there with a potentially net positive effect of biodiversity and ecological health. But in every setting, human life must revolve around being in close communication with the broader nonhuman community. "What are its needs?" must become "What are our needs?" for we are all one family sharing the same home.

Jon Andreas
Chino, California

Into the Ruins welcomes letters from our readers. We encourage thoughtful commentary on the contents of this issue, the themes of the magazine, humanity's future, and other relevant subjects. Readers may email their letters to editor@intotheruins.com or mail them to:

Joel Caris
Figuration Press
3515 SE Clinton Street
Portland, OR 97202

STORIES

WANTONLY AND RECKLESSLY

BY MIR SEIDEL

These events happened in the year 210 After Flooding.
They tell about the time before Tyana left her home and family
in New Charleston and began her wanderings.

TYANA LAY DEEP IN THE MANGROVE FOREST, suspended in a hammock of her own making. It was really her night-wrap, tied up in the tangle of air roots that reached out from their trunks like long skinny fingers to find the rising water under her. The cloth and the clawing roots made a cocoon for her, and a prison. She reached her arm out, sliding a hand down through the water to touch slick, rotting leaves, then brought it back up to wet her cracked lips. She needed to get up and make her way through the labyrinth of roots and branches to find water she could drink. She had been living outside, alone, for many days.

Last night the moon had spoken to her. Its face grew brighter and it began to talk, without a mouth, without words. It told her she would have to leave the forest. She should pay attention. Something would happen today.

Keisha stopped at the edge of the scrub pines to take in the long thread of beach below them. High tide was coming in. She shaded her eyes to look out at the cutting brightness of the water. The waves snaked up between the low straight lines of the roon walls, then hissed back down, carving channels like worm tracks in the sand. Sami, Keisha's little brother, had already launched himself down the bowl of the dune. He yelled, arms out, heels stomping into the sand. Keisha steeled herself for

27

the sun and followed him down the hill onto the beach.

Sami landed on his knees, got up and trotted to the nearest roon wall. He clambered up and walked along the ragged top, knocking the moss-bearded cinderblock with the long stick he'd picked up back in the pines. His basket flapped against the backs of his knees. Keisha scanned the sand for footprints, or even slight depressions, but all she saw was sandpiper tracks. If Ty had been here, there was no sign now. By the time Keisha caught up to Sami he was talking into his phone again.

"And guess what? We found a turtle! And Keisha says I can keep it for a pet!" Keisha gritted her teeth. None of this was true. And the phone was a lie too. It was just a hand-sized piece of metal Sami had found in what their father called the lost-and-found pile. Daddy had dug out part of a lower floor of the roon-building where they lived in the pine woods, and kept his different piles sorted down there out of sight: useful hardware like screws, nails, wires, and brackets; broken things for parts; and leftovers. She was pretty sure the "phone" was what her father called a switch-plate, but that didn't mean anything to Sami.

"Okay Daddy. Yes, I been real good." Sami held the thing out in front of him, like he could see his father in it. "I love you too! And guess what, me and Keisha and Ty are gonna come see you in Savannah!" Keisha's gut wrenched at the mention of their older sister. Sami jumped off the wall and walked across the sand, dragging the stick behind him. He climbed another roon wall, this one pointing down toward the water. A handful of tiny sanderlings ran back and forth in the wet line of the receding wave, their tracks softening and filling in. That's what Ty must have done —walked near the water so her tracks would disappear. Keisha drew her mouth tight and blinked back tears. It had been almost two weeks since she and Sami had found Ty lying on the beach, her face to the sky, waves washing up under her. They pleaded with her to come back home, but she just got up and ran away, her dress all wet and streaked with sand.

Ty had left three days after their parents set out on their spring trading circuit, down the coast to the Savannah settlements, and then moving inland on the way back. Her father offered his skills fixing fences, water pumps, and other metal things, in exchange for good hardware and unwanted or broken items. Mama did the negotiating, and oiled and sharpened tools.

Neither her mother nor her father had told Keisha she was in charge of her sister while they were away. Her dad told her to "hold the fort down," and her mom fixed her with a knowing look and said "I know you can do it." Meanwhile Ty sat in the corner, ignoring them, muttering to herself. It shouldn't be this way, with Keisha being ten and Ty already fifteen with grown-up breasts and having her period, but it was. Her parents couldn't take Ty along anymore. She had always been dreamy, leaving off in the middle of things, staring at nothing. On last year's trip she had wandered off and got lost a couple of times, and then started scaring the customers away with her yelling. Her fits didn't help either, even though everybody knew what to do when that happened, even Sami. They couldn't bring her, and they couldn't leave her home by herself. They had given Keisha the job of taking care of Ty, and she had lost her.

"Yeah, and know what?" Sami said. "I climbed on a really high wall, and I can see hella far! I can even see the Bridge from here!" The "really high" wall wasn't even up to Keisha's waist. Sami nodded at the metal plate. "Yes, I been minding Keisha." He must be talking to their mother now, that's something she would ask. Keisha moved away, walking alongside the sanderlings. She and Sami had started out from home after sun-up just to get through the pine woods, and they still had to go several more miles through the dunes, and then the mangroves, to get to the Testimony by noon.

That was the other thing. Her parents had set out later than usual, on account of the rains lasting longer. But Mama had promised they would be back in time for the Testimony. This would be the first time Keisha had to go without them. She and Sami could get along for a while: there was plenty of cornmeal left, and kelp. And they could bring back clams and oysters. Every day this last week she told Sami, "They're coming back tomorrow." At the same time, she would be picturing her parents and their big wheelbarrow surrounded by river gangers or just road robbers, who could take all the stuff they'd traded for, or their precious fixing tools, or worse. Her stomach balled up again.

A shadow moved over the waves. Keisha turned to see a spread of wings hanging dark against the sky. The bird eased down, wings still out, legs extended, to land in the shallow surf about fifty paces ahead. It was all white, an egret. Neck as long as her arm, crazy-thin stick legs that shouldn't be able to hold up its body, bending at odd angles. Towering over the sanderlings that rushed past it and back again, looking for whatever had attracted the bigger bird. Way out past the egret, she could just see the towers of Old Charleston shimmering in the water.

The egret staggered sideways, a crumple of wings, legs and neck. Sami gave a high whoop, standing on the wall, one fist held high. Keisha stormed over to him.

"Did you stone that bird?" she yelled, the tight knot inside her released into anger.

"I—I didn't . . ." His face changed, seeing hers. Keisha grabbed his arm and yanked him off the wall. He landed on hands and knees. The long stick flew out, bounced, then lifted in a big incoming wave and bobbed away as the wave receded. The bird had half-righted itself, and flew out at an angle, wings out of sync, croaking in distress.

"You don't know nothing! Come on!" This was not the time to be hunting a big bird like that. Keisha pulled him up by the elbow and steered him along roughly. Sami bawled. It felt more equal now to have him be miserable.

‡‡

Tyana had stayed on the beach many nights. Lying there, waiting. Listening to the waves, which had talked to her so much when she was a girl. But this time all they said was *Not yet, Not yet*. She stayed there, stubborn, feeling like a failure, with the sandflies biting her face, her arms and legs. She yelled up at the sky. Sometimes imps disguised as children came to harass her, calling her names, and poked her with sticks, their faces dark against the night. She roared at them, and they ran away laughing. Another night two more imp-children came, worse than the others because they knew her: they called her by name, crying, and pulled at her and begged her to come home with them. She jumped up, batted their arms off her and ran away. She had left the beach after that and went inland into the cabbage palm groves, where she ate the palm fruit and listened at night to the harsh whisper of leaves in the humid breeze. After a wildcat chased her up a tree, she moved on to the mangrove forest, slinging up her hammock when high tide rolled in.

Keisha and Sami picked their way through the mangrove forest. Grabbing trunks or branches when they could, then leaning out to balance their feet on another air-root. It was hard work—even under the canopy of trees, their bodies ran with sweat.

A black shadow swiveled slow in the water under them—a croc's tail, reminding them how careful they needed to be. Sami had already cut some oysters off the underside of a mangrove root, but now with the rising tide it was too dangerous. They were supposed to bring food to the Testimony, but their baskets were still light. Keisha couldn't worry about that now. She swept the wet hair off her forehead and swung herself onto the next root.

"I'm thirsty." Sami had stopped. He looked up at the leaves, neck bent so his halo of tiny curls fell backward. Keisha reached in her basket and pulled out the water tin. Sami took two careful gulps and handed it back. Keisha took one gulp. They went on, surrounded by the rustle of leaves and the harsh rising trill of the cicadas.

"There it is!" Sami yelled. Behind him, Keisha couldn't see anything through the thick-leaved overhang. Sami scrambled over several clumps of tree roots to get to the big overgrown roon, its low jagged walls half-eaten by the mangroves. Seeing it meant they were halfway through the forest. This roon was big in every direction; Daddy called roons like these "big boxes." He said that long ago they were giant markets with roofs over them that stayed lit up day and night, where hundreds of people came to buy things. Keisha tried to picture this, but couldn't.

Sami skipped along the zig-zagging tops of the roon-walls, pushing branches aside, jumping over air-roots that climbed around it. They passed the two huge metal poles that rose in front of the wall, higher than the tallest mangrove trees, so high you could see them from the other side of the pine woods where Keisha's family lived. There used to be a big banner hanging between the poles so people could see the name of the market from far away.

Sami had pulled his phone out again.

"Hi, Ty!" he called. Keisha tensed.

"Guess what, we're going to see Mama and Dad, in Savannah! Wanna come?"

She wanted to rip the metal thing away from him, but couldn't risk either of them falling into the brackish water. Sami held the phone in front of him, walking slower on the wall. "Okay. But where are you, anyhow? We been looking for you." He nodded, then turned back to Keisha.

"She says she's over that way." He tipped his head at an angle. Keisha was seized by the certainty that Sami was right—their sister was here, somewhere in the mangroves, inland from the big roon. They made their way past a warren of smaller walls that honeycombed in broken squares at the end of the long wall, and turned onto the side wall that led deeper into the forest. The trees bunched closer, blocking even more of the sun. Sami started calling Ty. Keisha couldn't help it—she started calling her sister's name too. Hearing their voices high and thinned out in the sticky air and almost drowned among the cicadas, she felt more and more desperate. Could Ty really be staying here, where the water rose twice a day?

"Please, Ty!" She felt herself growing smaller as she called. When they reached the end of the wall she stopped and shushed Sami. He turned back to look at her.

"You hear something?" he whispered. They stood still and listened.

"We're not gonna find her now." That was because Ty didn't want them to find her. "Let's go, maybe she'll follow us." Keisha grabbed onto a mangrove branch and stepped out onto a root, then reached back to help Sami jump off the wall. She'd been too hard on him before. They gave their full attention to their feet and hands, sweat dripping off them into the water.

Tyana lay in a spot of dank sand under the mangroves, her face swollen and hot. The leaves above her played hide-and-seek with the sun, some turning see-through yellow-green, then darker as they wove up and down in the faint breeze. Her mouth was dry, her eyelids caked.

Everything went quiet, even the far-off sea. Then all the leaves turned see-through in a widening circle of pale yellow light. She felt pinned to the ground, her breathing changed. The light kept growing till it surrounded her. She couldn't take it in—it took her in. Then the light spoke to her. Like the moon, it had no mouth or body, and its speaking was a kind of showing. The light gestured somehow, pulling her attention to the tangled web of mangrove roots all around, each one reaching for their own spot of ground. They were pale and colorless now, washed in the haze of light, but this made her see them all of a piece—uncounted filaments, weaving earth and sky together. Roots in the murk, leaves and twigs disappearing into the sky. All connected.

It's us, she thought. The light nodded, *Yes*. It was waiting for her to go on. *It's not them, it's us*, she told it. *Not just the Olders. The children too. All of us.* They were all connected, all equally responsible for what had happened before. Together, roots, branches, and leaves, no matter who came earlier or later.

The light expanded around her, a field of undifferentiated understanding, then found its way into her through every pore. She shivered and bucked on the sand, breathing the light in and out.

They stood blinking at the edge of the forest, looking out at the beach. Keisha reflexively pushed her hair forward so it bounced over her forehead, shielding her eyes from the hammering sunlight.

The beach had filled with people already. Standing here, a little higher than the sand, they could see straight out to the roons of Old Charleston. The broken towers gave off sprinkling shards of light, and the Bridge rose out of the water, glinting in the sun like a dream, then sinking back in on the other side. Some of its spokes still rayed up and around, looking thin as a spiderweb from here.

People were mostly facing toward the sea—the Testimony might be starting already, but Keisha couldn't see through to the shallows from here. Folks were still talking, and some little kids ran between the grownups, squealing. Keisha saw some of the Steptoes, and a bunch of Moultries, and some people she recognized from the New Charleston market. She looked for Dee Moultrie, who was about her age, but didn't see her. A lady gave her a funny stare as Keisha and Sami walked past her. Keisha pulled herself up straight and kept going. Had the lady had a run-in with Ty? Her mother would have said something to turn that stare away. Keisha realized she'd been holding out the hope that her parents would show up here, coming straight to the beach with their wheelbarrow and all.

The first "Whereas . . ." threaded out over the swashing waves—a woman's voice. Keisha picked her way on the wet sand, toward the sound.

". . . that we did wantonly and recklessly and with full forethought . . ." The old, strange words pierced her. Conversation died down, and the crowd joined in for the refrain. The Testimony made Keisha uncomfortable, but they'd always gone to it. She pushed and shimmied through knots of people till she could see the figures standing in the surf. Two men, one wiry and one beefy, both wearing shades. The wiry one wore a ganger band around his head, but that might just be for show.

Between them, they held up a tiny old woman by her bony arms. She was no taller than Keisha, and even skinnier—a little wave would knock her over if they weren't holding her. The blue shift she wore was already dark with seawater. Next to the wiry man stood a young woman. It was Shadda, a few years older than Tyana, wearing a halter top, her dark skin sparkling with spray. She held out a board with the words written on it, which meant she was the Speaker today. Even up this close, it was hard to hear her as she yelled out each phrase, then waited for the old woman to repeat it. The grandma's lips moved. She might have been saying something, but her eyes were vacant. Keisha listened, watching the speaker's mouth.

"Whereas we did conspire and siphoned out the black remains . . ." The music of the words came back to Keisha, even if she didn't understand most of it. The younger woman turned again to the grandma who moved her mouth like she was gumming on a hazelnut. Her face was scored by lines, she could have been sixty or even older. When Shadda looked ahead again, the crowd took up the final words, ". . . of long-dead creatures." Then she started in with another Whereas.

Another shout went up: ". . . created legions of infernal devices!" The call rippled from the front to the back, where they probably couldn't hear the speaker at all.

Keisha decided she would look away when they got to the end. Nobody here knew this decrepit old woman. The New Charleston gathering had an arrangement with another group up the coast, trading their oldest Older up there in exchange for one from here. Otherwise, their mother had explained to her, the Older's family might get too upset, or even try to interfere. This way, goodbyes could be said beforehand. But this woman might be a loner with no family.

"Whereas we did ignore and deny the growing fever of the earth . . ."

Keisha felt sick to her stomach. Her mother came from farther north, from one of the Wilmington settlements. One time after a Testimony, when Keisha was about Sami's age now, five or six, Mama got upset and angry. She said her old gathering was better, they just dunked the person under the waves for a minute, and usually they survived. Mama and Dad had argued about it. Dad said it was too dangerous to try to change things here.

". . . Whereas we did nothing while the waters rose and fires raged . . ."

Ty always got the most upset. She would refuse to look at the people in the water, and just stand turned away, crying, her face a fierce mask. The last few years they had let Ty stay home.

". . . wrought destruction." Hundreds of voices repeated and echoed the words. An arm rubbed Keisha's, and Sami leaned his head against her shoulder. Had he run away from her and come back? Keisha hadn't even noticed. She reached her arm around him and pulled him tight against her.

". . . Whereas our willful blindness, stubbornness and greed did lead the world into a dark time . . ."

The old woman had slowly drooped forward. Now her head almost touched the water. As the speaker leaned down to check her face, a wave rolled in high, splashing the men at mid-back and submerging the old woman. The men jerked her back up, too high—she dangled between them, legs loose, sputtering, gray hair flat against her tiny skull. Her eyes blinked open and she looked straight at Keisha, who couldn't look away. The eyes stabbed into her. They were asking Keisha a question, something she couldn't answer. Another refrain rose behind her, but she didn't hear the words. Then there was a waiting silence. Shadda's voice rang out, starting the last part:

"Wherefore, before all gathered here . . ."

Behind them someone yelled. Keisha couldn't see but knew it was Ty. She craned backward toward the mangroves, and started pushing between bodies.

"Stop! You're wrong!" Ty was saying. She must have run down the sand, around the crowd, to the water line. Now Keisha saw her, striding along the sand, still bellowing. Ty was covered in mud—it streaked her face, legs, and arms, and thickened in her locks. Her gray eyes wide, lips cracked, scratches and sandfly-welts all over her exposed skin.

"Y'all don't know what you're doing!" she yelled, facing the crowd. A man broke away and lunged toward her. At the same time Sami darted out, calling to Ty. He collided with the man, throwing the grownup's trajectory off just enough that Ty was able to swerve out of his reach. The man stumbled and threw Sami backward on the sand. He lay there, mouth open, staring up at the sky. Somehow Keisha was there next to him, screaming.

Sami took a jagged breath, then started to howl.

Ty stalked ahead, kicking through the waves toward where the men held up the old lady. The speaker had recovered from the interruption, and started reciting again.

". . . do freely admit these heinous wrongdoings perpetrated on our descendants . . ."

Ty shouted over her, still addressing the people on shore.

"Look what you're doing!"

". . . knowing that remorse for our actions is not enough . . ."

Ty shouldered in between the speaker and the guy with the headband.

"The hell!" the speaker shouted. "Dewey! Do something!"

"Don't you see it?" Ty shouted, wheeling her arms up and around her. Dewey let go of the old woman and reached to grab Ty by her wrists. Ty backed deeper into the waves, but he wrestled her back into line with the others.

"It's all of us!" Ty cried out, her voice loud and rough. "Not just her!" Her head flicked toward the old woman. Dewey had pulled Ty's wrists behind her with one hand, and with the other, pushed her head down toward the water.

"You let her go!" Keisha yelled, running out into the waves toward Ty, as her sister twisted against the man and kept shouting.

"Stop it, I'm trying to explain—"

Keisha grabbed the man's near arm with both hands, leaned in and bit as hard as she could, tasting salt and blood. Roaring, the man jammed his arm into Keisha's face. She fell back in the water, and a wave rolled over her, flooding down her throat and pushing her body back and away, till her back scraped the sand. She pushed herself up to sitting, choking and spitting up seawater.

Sami had splashed back through the water, and threw himself at the bigger man, climbing up his arm and onto his back. Keisha staggered back toward them as the man reached to pull Sami off. Keisha tackled him, hugging around his giant chest. Everything teetered, and she fell backward into the water, with the man weighing down on her like the keel of a boat. She rolled sideways into bubbles and wave-wash, and fought her way up into the air.

Ty was standing, still yelling, facing the crowd, her arms out, water streaming off her, all the mud washed off her shining skin. Keisha scanned around her for Sami —he stood in the water behind her, retching up water.

The speaker and the thinner man, Dewey, stood together, looking in the water, where the old woman lay face down, arms and legs sinking down. They'd lost track of her in the confusion. Now she'd gone and died without ever getting to say the last part. Ty had ruined it. And she didn't care. Ty didn't care if she herself lived or died.

Keisha watched, feeling separate from what she saw, her body weightless as a leaf. She knew what she had to do: stand near enough to Ty to remind people that she was part of a family too. Watch her sister for the first sign that she was slowing down. Edge toward her, and without saying anything, take her arm. Then, if the others let them, she would lead her sister gently home.

This story is told of Tyana: how she felt a great restlessness that made her remove herself from others. She lived for a time in the forests and marshes, eating only fruits and leaves. She spoke only to the turtles and the egrets who waded there.

On the day of the old ceremony that was held once a year at the high tide after the summer solstice, Tyana received a visit from a spirit who enlightened her and commanded her to pass along what she had learned. And so she took herself to the ceremony and began to speak. She went in the water and took the speaking-board from the speaker, and threw it far out into the sea. And she took the old woman who had been chosen, and lifted her up and carried her onto the shore and laid her down.

Then she told the people of New Charleston how they should end the practice of that day, because We Are All Responsible and not just the Olders, that Olders and

Youngers are part of the same whole, roots, branches, and leaves. But the others shouted and jeered and pulled at her, even including her own sister and brother. Because at this time no one understood the message she brought. And Tyana knew then that she would have to leave this place, and go tell others what she had learned. This happened as we have described.

THE LIGHT OF MENTORS

BY DEVON MARSH

I WALK OUTSIDE AFTER DARK AND CAN'T SEE THE STARS. Not in this bright town. Our own radiance obscures our view. Which is ironic, I suppose, but that's where we are. A few stars sometimes manage to shine through. Sirius would be visible later in the year. Now, I should be able to see Alshain, but I can't see it in all this scattered light. No one can, even though it's right there, just above my building.

Oh, my. My building. Not just the place where I work, but the place where I was working then. Then being now, when we completed years of analysis and made our announcement. And I led the team. If this wins a prize, they might actually name this building for me. Like Michelson Hall, with its row of bronze disks marking the path a beam of light followed when Albert Michelson measured its speed.

I spent a lot of hours sitting in classrooms in Michelson, wondering what I'd gotten myself into at the Naval Academy. Wondering if I could make it through a physics degree. Even wondering what it had been like for Michelson as a nine-teenth-century Midshipman, and then as a naval officer and scientist. Looking back, it's clear to me I drew some inspiration from him, from his youth, and the magnitude of his accomplishment. It made him the first American to win the No-bel Prize. I suppose he was a distant mentor, because here I am. And I still wonder just like I did back then: where is that beam now? A hundred and thirty-something light years away. It could have traveled to Alshain and back and to Alshain again in that length of time. The beginning of a conversation.

I don't know if I'd ever get over it if they named this building for me. Or if not this one, the one that someday replaces it. Not because what we did wasn't momen-tous, just that in retrospect it seems so simple. And what we learned, so sad.

The simple part is that we have it, the first evidence. All the data, all the analy-sis, all the proof. Tomorrow we'll tell the world. Whether the world hears the message or not is a different story. This story—the story of our discovery—has come to an end. It began before I was born. It began with SETI.

The projects we call SETI—the Search for Extraterrestrial Intelligence—date back to 1960. Even before then, both Tesla and Marconi imagined this type of work. I'm sure neither of them appreciated it would be like searching for a needle in a haystack. From the outset of the modern project, when Frank Drake collected signals with a radio telescope in West Virginia, program administrators knew the challenge lay not in collecting signals. Collection was easy. Instead, the challenge lay in separating signal from noise. Data processing power was the key to discovering a signal in all the collected noise. Without noise, artificial signals would be easy to recognize. They would be repetitive, though probably irregular, and they would occupy narrow bandwidths. Some pattern, however faint, however unfamiliar, would surely differ from background phenomena in a way that would allow SETI algorithms to discern signal from noise. Yet year after year, they didn't. Therefore more processing power was brought to bear.

In the late twentieth century, mainframe computers offered the muscle necessary to run complex noise-filtering algorithms, but they did so at great expense. To increase processing power without increasing expense, program administrators settled on the idea of distributed computing. They adopted the approach in 1999 when SETI enlisted idle desktop computers around the world. Volunteers signed on to let their machines run SETI algorithms during periods of low use. Each participant must have hoped the first string of alien text, the first line of conversation, or the first broadcast greeting from another planet might run through their computer, be detected, and vault the citizen-scientist to fame.

In addition to distributed processing, SETI developed methods to employ backyard satellite dishes as modestly sensitive radio telescopes. This supplemented Project Argus, a SETI affiliate that coordinates a global network of small, amateur-built radio telescopes in an effort to achieve real-time coverage of the entire sky. The sensitivity of these collectors is as good as that of the Ohio State Big Ear antenna that detected the "Wow!" signal in 1977.

Dreamers with antennas and computers signed up for both of these programs. They joined hoping to hear an otherworldly Edison hollering "Mary had a little lamb" from somewhere out in space. Hundreds of thousands of volunteers provided hundreds of teraflops of processing power. Still, the needle, if there was one, remained in the hay.

In 2004, I worked with a team of graduate students who were good at discerning signal from noise in a different field of haystacks. Our field lay not in the sky but here on earth. We had a grant to examine audio recordings collected by drone aircraft. We intended to process the sound similar to the way operators of SOSUS arrays processed acoustic recordings to detect submarine signatures. Instead of detecting mechanical sounds in the ocean, we sought ways to capture conversations traveling through the air. We hoped to make it possible to glean intelligence with expendable, unmanned aircraft rather than costly, vulnerable human assets on the ground.

Our team designed an array of microphones attuned to the frequency range of the human voice. We employed simple filtering techniques to cancel out the 50- and 60-Hertz hum of electrical components, the thousand-rpm drone of the aircraft's propellers, and the ten thousand-rpm whine of its engines. We did all of this with technology as common as that found in the noise-canceling headphones many of us wear on long commercial flights. We canceled the noise and we listened for the signal, and we found no needles in the haystack. Undeterred, we believed in our purpose and our method, so we refined our techniques. I told the team to construct algorithms to attract likely data sets the way a magnet dragged through hay would attract a needle. I assured them this was how we would succeed. I was wrong.

Insight comes from unlikely sources. One evening during a dinnertime conversation of "Did you know?" and "Oh, yeah? Well did YOU know?" that makes up part of my family's mealtime ritual, my youngest son told the rest of us about early settlers moving west. "Do you know the last thing they did when they moved?" he asked. No one answered. "They burned their cabins." He beamed as we sat wondering why in the world anyone would destroy their home, especially one they had built themselves through great expenditure of energy and precious resources. After a moment my son added, "To recover the nails." I got up from the dinner table and walked to my computer to email my students. We didn't need a magnet to attract the needle. To find the needle, we needed to burn the hay.

Within minutes, I had two responses. The first came from our resident naysayer. The Fun-Vacuum, we called him, for his ability to deflate many a sense of elation with his irritating voice of reason. "A relatively dense needle will sink into ashes and remain hidden," he wrote. He could even suck the fun out of a metaphor.

Seconds later, our unconstrained freethinker responded. "Burn the hay and ignore needles. Look for spikes instead."

So we ignored the noise, ignored metaphorical needles, and wrote an algorithm for spikes. Literally, spikes in signal intensity. We ignored the noise through time compression of our samples, burning away what we had once examined for snippets of conversation. What remained was a monotonous undercurrent of sped-up noise, punctuated by spikes of sound. In previous analysis, these spikes had not even caught our interest because they weren't what we were looking for. They weren't voices. Yet now they stood out as clearly as iron spikes lying in the ashes of a burned cabin. We picked them up, turned them over, examined the recordings in real time, and recognized that the spikes were man-made. They were as man-made as angry shouts and just as charged with emotion, but they weren't voices at all. They were gunfire.

Our ability to detect gunfire in recordings captured by drone aircraft was a first step. In the early recordings we analyzed, the gunfire led us to detect voices associated with skirmishes. That detection, and subsequent analysis of actual voices captured by test drones in real-world conditions, helped us refine our techniques. We improved both our detection and our analysis. At the same time, drone technology advanced considerably. Now drones are smaller, quieter, more agile than ever. They can go places and record sounds that we would not have thought possible a decade ago. As a result, voice detection has become routine.

We continue to make advances, and we have a voracious customer for the product of our efforts. I can't describe the current state of this technology in too much detail, nor can I comment on its uses. However when you are talking with a partner in a pastoral setting with no one else in sight, and you feel free to speak your mind or your heart amidst birdsong and the whisper of wind through the trees, be romantic and brash. Feel free to strip naked and run through the grass. You may be seen, but don't worry about that. Just be careful what you say.

But I'm getting off track. When we think of gunfire, it's useful to consider its iconic forms. The report of a rifle, the boom of a shotgun. The roar of cannon, the whine of a bullet, even the unheard sound of the one that gets you. We know a burst of automatic weapons fire, the *pop-pop-pop* of a drive-by. We also know iconic shots in history. In 1775, a colonial soldier fired "the shot heard 'round the world." And one hundred seventy years later, the United States set off what we could call "the shot heard across the stars."

The EM pulse from the blast at Trinity Site in New Mexico was of an intensity that dwarfed radio transmissions of the day. To a radio telescope observer within a few light years of earth, it would have stood out from interstellar noise like a spike rising from a background of unremarkable ash. Anyone in this part of our galaxy may yet hear that shot, as well as the many that followed. My team and I heard just such a shot. To our astonishment, it was fired by someone else.

The SETI Project has done remarkable work. Since its inception, it has considered thousands of spurious signals emanating from near and distant sources in space. All of those have been examined and discounted. The "Wow!" signal and all the other tantalizing leads have fizzled. Yet the project has compiled an extensive collection of recordings. Of noise, really, at least by the standards of the time. However, the collection provides a valuable archive, full of potential for further exploration. It is a vast field of hay raked and shocked into neat stacks awaiting someone who wants to search for needles. Or spikes.

Public funding for SETI ceased in 1994. Private funding has sustained it ever since, subject to the vicissitude of donors. The project has survived on a shoestring budget. In contrast, my project to enhance the detection capabilities of unmanned aircraft, deemed crucial to national security, remains well funded. In addition, our work has resulted in patents that have produced a significant stream of income. As a result, we are flush with funds. It was a non-issue for us to come up with enough money to offer a generous donation to SETI in return for a look at its archive. Its director granted our request even though we were out of our element entirely. We must have seemed like some rich agricultural historian offering an irresponsible but welcome donation to an art museum in exchange for a closer look at Van Gogh's haystacks.

In 2011 my team began to examine SETI data, but not before the Fun-Vacuum expressed reservations. In dismal emails, he wrote, "Our algorithms are written for base frequencies in hundreds and low thousands of Hertz, not Megahertz and above. Their scalability is non-linear . . ." And, "Cultural phenomena that would constitute locally-intense events are unlikely, whereas your metaphorical spikes are relatively common in crude frontier cabins." Yet despite his stilted pessimism, the naysayer adapted our algorithms with alacrity. In a matter of weeks, we were processing SETI data. In a month, we heard gunfire.

I can't help but marvel at the technological evolution that's evident here. Someone decades ago wrote programs on punch cards, recorded them on magnetic tapes, and ran them to detect Cold War submarines in sound captured by undersea microphones. My team adapted that code to detect sounds of interest intercepted by remotely controlled aircraft. We stored the modified code on compact disks. Just a few years later, it served as the basis for still newer code which we now store on flash drives. We run it to scan interstellar noise as we look for signs of intelligent life. That just amazes me. But this story is not about human technological evolution. No, this is the story of someone else, a people with a history all their own, and we heard them.

First, we heard their gunfire. Or at least a shot. Beginning with the earliest SETI records, we scanned more than twenty years of data in a few weeks. We soon detected a spike. Captured in 1981, the spike resembled the electromagnetic burst one would expect to see from an uncontrolled fission reaction. Spectral analysis indicated it involved Uranium-235. This captivated us, because fissile reactions of U-235 are rare in nature.

The signal that included our spike emanated from the region of the star known as Alshain. Astronomers catalog it as the second-brightest star in the constellation Aquila, giving it the designation Beta Aquilae. Aquila, the eagle, lies along the Milky Way just north of the celestial equator. It is visible during the summer. While Alshain shines in our sky as part of Aquila, an observer in that star system looking in our direction would see Sol, our own sun, as part of Canis Major, the dog that accompanies Orion the Hunter. To the residents of the third planet of Alshain, our sun would form the ear of the dog. And sure enough, here we are, listening.

Alshain lies forty-five light years from our solar system. Given that distance, and considering the date on which the signal arrived at earth, it's easy to refer to the earth-year in which specific events on the other planet transpired. As we consider time and measures of time, it is interesting to note that the planet Three Beta Aquilae to which we localized our spike has a day lasting twenty-nine hours, and it completes an orbit of Alshain in two hundred ninety-eight of its days. Although the distribution of daylight hours differs from ours, the amount of time in a year on that world differs from the amount of time in one of our own years by only two hours. A remarkable coincidence? Of course it is. And it's one of many facts available for further consideration.

The signal we detected left its home planet in 1936. Our team saw another spike in SETI data from later that same year, and it also emanated from Three Beta Aquilae. This spike bore characteristics very similar to the first, down to the spectral lines from a fissile reaction of U-235. Intensity was slightly greater, but not remarkably so.

We didn't locate other spikes in SETI data until more than a year later. Logs of the source data collected during the intervening period reveal that Beta Aquilae, or Alshain, was not included in surveys during most of that time. However when we did detect another spike, it came from Alshain. This third spike occurred in 1941. Its intensity was noticeably greater, although within the same order of magnitude of the first two. A key difference, though, lay in spectral lines. They indicated a fissile reaction of Plutonium-238. If we can draw an inference from mankind's own experience, it suggests we are seeing evidence of technological evolution. This particular evolution is unfortunate.

History repeats itself, even within the microcosm of our little project. In our work with drone aircraft, we first looked for spikes of sound as a proxy for human activity. In the data close to the gunfire captured in our audio recordings, we sharpened our analysis until we detected human voices. Eventually we refined our techniques enough to detect voices outright, without the need for gunfire to draw our attention. We followed a similar progression in our analysis of SETI data.

Our goal, and the goal of the SETI project from the outset, was detection of a modulated radio signal. A carrier signal, laden with whatever information a broadcaster chose to impart. We refined our computational routines to the point that we could detect the signals we sought, but the sensitivity of our algorithms was not the only limitation in detecting radio transmissions. The intensity of the broadcast and the sensitivity of our hardware posed physical obstacles to detection.

A basic assumption of early SETI work was that limitations in detection would enable us to receive only a strong, overt signal explicitly transmitted for the purpose of contacting an intelligent listener. What mattered more than our ability to recognize a signal from an intelligent source was our technological ability to detect it at all. Assuming the use of the most sensitive receivers available, detection is limited by the "effective isotropically radiated power" of the transmitter, or EIRP. That's the amount of power an antenna would have to emit to produce a signal observable by a receiver of sufficient sensitivity. Our detection of a deliberate transmission depended on having receivers sensitive enough to receive and record signals of reasonable EIRP, weakened by spherical spreading over interstellar distances. Technical enhancements and improvements in receivers now give us the ability to detect a signal transmitted with an intensity of less than one gigawatt EIRP transmitted within two hundred light years. But that sensitivity was much lower until quite recently. This means if anyone was saying anything before now, we probably missed what they said.

About six years ago SETI completed a significant upgrade to the sensitivity of its detective equipment. Right after the upgrade, the project captured a large quantity of data from the region of Aquila. A few weeks ago our team processed that data, using algorithms refined beyond the point of detecting spikes. What we found thrilled us: a modulated radio signal carrying evidence of intelligent civilization. That still amazes me. We had realized the SETI program's goal—and one of mankind's dreams.

While we couldn't translate into words what we heard on audio renderings of the signal, what we did hear and see in the data was obvious. We saw an embellishment of the carrier frequency repeated at intervals throughout the twenty-nine hour day of planet Three Beta Aquilae. The sounds remind me of the fanfare that was prelude to the BBC World Service broadcasts I listened to on shortwave radio as a young man. It was the Lilliburlero, the signature introduction that played after tones counted down to the hour and the solemn announcer said, "THIS is London." Maybe the network still does that, I don't know. Anyone who has heard it knows exactly what I mean. Or maybe people are more familiar with the eight-note tune we hear each afternoon on the way home from work at the beginning of "All Things Considered" on NPR. That is exactly what we have in these recordings from the third planet of Alshain in the constellation Aquila. We have the news. Without a Rosetta stone we may never understand the broadcast, but it's the news.

I suspect the news was grim. We detected bursts of electromagnetic radiation from Alshain's third planet. The bursts bore characteristic signs of explosive fissile reactions. The first blasts involved Uranium-235, while other early explosions involved Plutonium-238. Blasts followed a semi-regular pattern consistent with the sort of nuclear testing the United States and the Soviet Union engaged in during the mid-twentieth century. Then, after about seven years of fission explosions on Three Beta Aquilae, we saw evidence of a much more intense EM pulse. The explosion bore signs of a fusion reaction produced by a hydrogen bomb. It even had the telltale tritium hyperfine line at 1516 MHz. SETI researchers have long regarded the tritium frequency as interesting because the isotope is rare, and because emission may indicate nuclear fusion carried out by a technologically advanced civilization. Looks like they were right.

The fusion explosions we detected continued in a regular pattern, as did further fission explosions. Peak intensity of occasional blasts increased significantly. The more routine blasts settled at five distinct levels. Team members draw different inferences from this observation. A prevailing thought is that these levels represent mass-production tactical and strategic weapons of prescribed yield being tested as part of a weapons development program. Explosions involving these devices continued through about fifteen years' worth of data, until they stopped.

The EM pulses we detected left us with no doubt. We were observing artifacts of an advanced civilization. We were fairly certain it had not directed a strong signal our way, although there were gaps in our data from periods during which no observations of the region around this star had been recorded. The data that contained the news broadcasts excited us beyond our wildest expectations. We had been at this for mere months at that point, having reprocessed all SETI data ever captured using detection algorithms that we continually refined. When we made a significant improvement, we re-ran data we had run just days earlier. We were no longer looking at the entire SETI archive, just the data for Beta Aquilae. The nuclear tests stopped, we endured a few days of signals captured on older receivers, and then we processed data captured after the 2006 upgrade. Right away we detected the flourish of music that I am sure came as prelude to a program of some type. I would not have been surprised to hear, "THIS is Alshain." Instead, we heard another shot.

Two data-processing days after the radio signal we call the News Program, we detected a fission explosion of modest intensity. We wondered if explosions like it had been taking place all along and had simply fallen into gaps in the recorded data. Or maybe the blasts had been suspended under a test ban treaty. Whatever the case, we had not seen spikes in several years' worth of data, and now we found one. Meanwhile, we detected other news programs. We recorded enough to see a pattern emerge. And we recorded another fission explosion. Then another.

One week after processing the first data records captured with equipment installed in the upgrade, we detected a fusion explosion. An hour's worth of data later, another. Thirty minutes later, we recorded the first of four hundred thirty-eight large fusion explosions that detonated within a twenty-minute window. Then silence, until we detected one lone transmission.

The transmission that followed the period of intense explosive activity was a modulated carrier signal bearing a message that repeats at precise intervals. Its periodicity led us to conclude that it comes not from the third planet of Alshain, rather from a moon of that planet. The transmitter sits on the side of the moon facing away from the planet, shielded from all of the EM bursts that would have rendered ground-based and orbital transmitters useless.

Today, after transmitting continually for six years, the modulated signal still emanates from a moon of the third planet of Alshain. We see it routinely in the data, unaccompanied by other transmissions of any kind from that planetary system. The signal carries only a single phrase, repeated around the clock. Beyond any doubt the transmission is automated, not live.

The automated transmission may be all that remains of a civilization that flourished forty-five light years from here. Members of its society might have looked up into the night sky toward Orion and Canis Major and seen an unremarkable star above Sirius forming the point of the great dog's ear. The observers may have wondered if life existed on planets orbiting the stars they saw. They could not have known that by now, signs of our civilization would be reaching theirs. And even if they had guessed or speculated that someday they would detect us, they would not have guessed that the first person to know about them would tell our world about the inhabitants of Alshain-3 in the past tense, reporting that evidence of their civilization resides now only in recorded data. Live evidence sped past us years ago. It is already light years away and receding, fading as it expands. It will not be detected again.

We may never know what the remaining transmission from Alshain says. I think it calls out from the collapsed universe of its own world to the expanse of neighboring space, asking a single question over and over again. It's the same question humans have wondered since we first looked up, since we first began to listen to the stars, as attuned as a dog who has cocked an ear to the cry of an eagle. We ask, "Is anyone there?"

I remember walking out of class onto the plaza between Michelson and Chauvenet Halls at the Naval Academy. No matter how much of a hurry I might have been in to get to my next class or to noon meal formation or to go on liberty with my friends, I always looked at the row of brass disks set in the conglomerate paving tiles. I let my gaze follow the path they memorialized. When the crowd of midshipmen and tourists was thin, and certainly if I was alone, I would walk along the line defined by those disks. I followed the path of a beam of light ignited by my distant mentor, and I wondered where it led, where its photons were at that moment. They're out there somewhere, faint and undetectable. But there, like the evidence of Alshain. Alshain's photons are the light of mentors, gone forever with the lessons they might have shared.

"Hope lies in the children"

by Dewey Dabbar

THIS LATE OCTOBER DAY—for those experiencing it in Pokeyhole, Connecticut (population 11,138)—was overcast with a chill in the air. These were conditions more likely to prompt a coffee-and-donut stop than to inspire any great change in direction. Maybe if a solar fire had warmed the souls heading up the hill to the red-brick town hall then they would have been bolder in that afternoon's meeting on the environment. Or maybe such taking-charge would have required both a bright sun and for Bill Buckner to have fielded that ball up the line a half hour after midnight. Pokeyhole, which was closer to Boston than New York, was very much within the territory of the newly coined "Red Sox Nation." And its baseball-loving populace was groggy with a hangover of disbelief from the previous night's game.

Above the grand doorway through which the town hall's afternoon visitors entered, the American flag tugged ever-so-gently at its pole. A bird perched on that brass-effect cylinder could, on a clear day, look down across the valley of the Connecticut River.

The town's environmental group had been brought together by local politician Marty Goodthinker, who drew a private pleasure from serving in his state's least Reagan-leaning congressional district. News of the hole in the ozone layer the previous year had got Marty out of his seat. But it was the recent disaster at Chernobyl that had settled his mind on forming the group, which was something he found himself able to do thanks to the behind-the-scenes support of a trio of concerned citizens. These three assembled with Marty and eight others at the town hall that afternoon.

While Marty silently read through his notes for a final time, the other group members found seats and waited for their heart rates to slowly ease back down from the upward jolt of the hill climb. Their conversation centered on the World Series, the deciding game of which had been postponed, after a downpour at Shea Stadium, from that evening to the next.

"I just don't know how you come back from something like that," offered a woman with dark hair streaming out from under a cap that bore an embroidered B.

"McNamara should have pulled Buckner after the top of the tenth," opined a man in a checked shirt, who was a recent college graduate. "Anyone can see his ankles are shot."

"If they don't win tomorrow," announced another cap-wearer, a sun-beaten man in his late fifties, "I swear I'm gonna switch to ice hockey. I just can't handle this anymore."

The one person, besides Marty, not inputting into the conversation was Angela Makepeace, a member of the local politician's supporting tripod. The only sport in which she took any interest was skeet shooting. And so, as others fretted about Game 7 and what the extra day's rest might mean for the respective rotations, Angela conducted a mental search for a witty introduction. She spotted an opportunity in the group's circular seating arrangement.

"Thank you. . . . Thank you for coming along this afternoon," announced Marty, in a raised voice, over fading chatter. "Let's start by introducing ourselves. Who wants to go first?"

"Okay! My name is Angela. And I'm an environmentalist."

On another day, in another town, this might have received generous laughter, but only Marty responded audibly to the parallel drawn by Angela, and he quickly stifled his own reaction as he sensed the majority feeling.

The introductions resumed.

"Hi," said the sun-beaten man, who was next in the circle. "I'm Dave, and I'm a local resident. I came here today because I'm getting more and more concerned about the state of the planet. And I want to know what politicians are going to do about it."

"Thank you, Dave," said Marty through a restrained wince. This particular politician had enough on his plate already. The meeting, for him, was meant to be about empowering the citizenship.

"Hi, I'm Gabriella, and I'm also a local resident. I'm worried about what kind of planet we're leaving behind for our kids. That's why I came today."

And so they continued. After everyone had said something about themselves, Marty steered the meeting through a critique of the damage that humans are doing to the Earth, then away from political action, and, finally, in a more stuttering fashion, toward the need for citizen action. At this point, the sun-beaten man —with his concern, like the discussion's momentum, having waned markedly —pulled out a magazine from his bag and began to read. The result of this action was the direction toward him of several razor-sharp glares, expressions of a kind that might, typically, have been reserved for someone flinging dog muck around.

Struggling to overcome this potential death knell, the group fell silent for a while, until Angela made a proposal that not only was greeted with warm and unanimous support but lightened the spirits of those present.

"It's clear that adults cannot behave responsibly. . . . We have to look to the next generation to make things right. . . . Hope lies in the children."

Billy Sanchez, a heavyset man with a shaven head and raven moustache, was a lifelong resident of Pokeyhole, Connecticut (population 19,554). He had been born in the local hospital in the first hour of October 26, 1986. While his mother had been paying full attention to the birth-giving process, his father was glued to a waiting-room TV that was showing replays of a small white orb slipping between a man's legs and into right field.

Billy was celebrating his forty-fourth birthday with a late lunch at a table for one in the Pilgrim Bar & Grill, and his beloved Red Sox were a game away from another championship. He loved this team because, above all else, watching them brought back fond memories of his youth, when he stayed up late to watch his co-heroes, Nomar Garciaparra and Pedro Martinez, exuding brilliance. During those years he had divided his backyard emulations between these two alone. A secondary-level hero, hard-hitting catcher Jason Varitek, was honored in a different way. He had his bobblehead figure glued to the top of the family recycling bin that had been installed at Billy's request. Every time a soda can was thrown in, the catcher's plastic head would wobble gleefully.

What has happened to my motivation to make the world a greener place? What has gone wrong with the sport I cherished so dearly? As a partial answer to this second question, Billy was aware of the harm that commercialism had inflicted on his relationship with baseball. Beyond that, he struggled to explain how his passions of youth could have fizzled like they had. That being said, they were not all dead. This was a World Series. And Samuel Lopez was capping off an explosive year with a postseason for the ages.

Lopez would be taking the hill in Game 6 and going for a World Series record fourth win, following victories in Games 1, 3, and 5. (As long as the league resisted extending the Series to a best-of-nine format, this was one of the rare records in the game that would truly be unbeatable.) The ace's immediate return to the mound was enabled by the four- and five-day breaks in the Series for jet-lag adjustment, which had been introduced as part of the resolution to the players' strike of 2028. While the league had presented that move as being a concession to the players, they privately knew that it would only help their revenue line, because it would permit extra ace-versus-ace matchups and allow six of the seven potential games to fall on the weekend. This last point was made especially important by the large time difference between the States—especially its West Coast markets—and the bases of the two European franchises. The working day, as the league's data made abundantly clear, really interfered with advertising revenue.

The Amsterdam Architects and the London Olympians were created in 2027, as expansion teams to the eastern divisions of the senior and junior circuit, respectively. To facilitate success on the field and thus encourage rapid growth off the field in their home countries, both teams had been granted an increased salary cap for their first ten years and were given four more pre-September roster spots than all their competitors. Simultaneously to this monumental change in the league's global footprint, its administrators reduced the distance between the mound and the plate from sixty feet and six inches to fifty-six feet and six inches. (Many bloggers aired suspicions that this coincidental timing was intended to deflect attention away from the latter and thus lessen the ire of purists.) While the average length of half-innings fell significantly as a result of this pitcher-favoring shift, longer breaks between them ensured that games were still of a "traditional length"—these words being quoted from a league press release.

Even with creative scheduling being employed to soften the time difference, both European franchises enjoyed a substantial home-field advantage. Furthermore, they were able to lessen the hindrance of road games by maintaining a separate pitching staff in the States and Europe. They only flew pitchers in either direction for the tail-end of lengthy home stands or road trips. North American teams had protested about the advantages enjoyed by the Architects and the Olympians. However, the projected increase in revenue to be shared across teams—at a time of great financial pressure on a game increasingly felt to be too slow for the modern age —won the argument for the league. Now, one of the European teams was, for the first time, contesting a World Series. And much of the wealthier part of Red Sox Nation had flown out to Schiphol, then back to New England, and then out again.

Somewhere, deep down, Billy felt that this whole thing was just wrong. As he waited for his lunch order, which he'd placed using his personal device, he searched the internet for a copy of the league's green policy. Finding it, he saw it mention that "the increased carbon expenditure had been largely offset by offering an expanded range of vegan options at ballparks, through improved composting methods of food waste, and via an increased rollout of LED technology and solar panels." *Now that is some creative accounting*, thought Billy. The policy also spoke of "an openness to foreground green transport technologies as they came online to ensure the ongoing environmental sustainability of the league." *I thought someone said that solar power would never be able to get planes off the ground*, Billy mused.

In Game 6, Lopez got a shutout win. Shortly after the final out, Billy slid off his bar stool, made a trip to the bathroom, and then headed out into the fading sun of a late afternoon. The initial sensation of cold as he emerged was quickly reversed on his walk up the hill toward Pokeyhole's fine town hall. There was a meeting taking place there that had been convened by a branch of the Concerned Citizens of Connecticut. Billy knew about it because it had been advertised on a digital screen above his favored urinal at the Pilgrim. Retinal scanning by a reader in the screen logged that Billy had viewed the whole ad, and he thus qualified for a discount on his next drink. (The accuracy of urinal users at the Pilgrim had never been poorer.)

The gathering had been in full swing for an hour when Billy arrived. Stepping over the legs of a sleeping man who looked to Billy to be in his seventies, he quietly settled into a seat in the back row and slowly repaid the breathing debt that he'd taken out on the climb. The sleeping man was one of the few people not grasping a personal device. These days, when time was in such short supply, only dinosaurs considered it impolite for someone to double-, triple-, or quadruple-task in a public meeting.

On sitting down, Billy quickly felt a need to take off his outer layer as he had inadvertently positioned himself in the trajectory of the room's rear air conditioner. Elsewhere, people retained their jackets—perhaps, Billy thought, because of the two open windows near the front. Once comfortable, the newcomer allowed his mind to ease itself into the toing and froing of voices, as he stroked the thick, dark hair above his lips. Billy's foray detected a fair bit of anger, a good deal of blame apportioning, and a regular stream of point-scoring via the citing of statistics, as if the Olympics was taking place and the blue ribbon event was knowing very precise things about ecological decline.

A half-hour after his arrival—and immediately following a tense moment in which a young woman named Isabella Grunter, representative for a group called Smaller Families for Sustainability, had been shot down simultaneously from several angles—there was a silent pause . . . and Billy thrust his hand up into it.

"Yes, the person at the back," said the gathering's principal convener through a lapel mike, with evident relief at the opportunity to shift the meeting away from the topic of overpopulation. "I don't think you've spoken yet, have you? Could you start by saying who you are, please."

"I'm Billy, and I'm . . . I guess . . . a concerned local."

"And what point would you like to make, Billy?"

"I've been listening to the discussion, and it seems to me that the adults in the town, me included, can't be trusted to do right by the planet. The politicians are doing nothing nearly dramatic enough to change things, and neither are we. But there is a hope. And it's to this we must turn our attention if the planet is going to be saved. . . . Hope lies in the children."

Rarely had an opinion voiced in that room been met with such enthusiastic agreement.

‡‡

Anna Firkin was born in the fall of 2030 and had spent almost all of the subsequent forty-nine years and eleven months, up to the present day, in the eastern North American town of Pokeyhole (estimated population 5,000). She reflected on her upcoming milestone birthday, and the streaks of gray in her long chestnut hair, as she climbed the hill to the town hall effortlessly. The ease of this activity was not unusual in a society that had reverted to so much manual activity. Anna was especially fit, though. The lockable closet in her squat house contained no skeletons, but it did hold an old lycra running outfit that she wore for her secret celestially lit jogs in the scrubbed-over field margins to the east of Pokeyhole. Anna had not managed to become a property owner before the start of the age of collapse, but with the declining population, many old residences now stood available for unofficial tenants. The prime residences were those that had not been extended beyond their original size, as these were the ones, generally, that remained sturdy and watertight. Squats were preferred over individual or dual occupancy because the safety in numbers—against looters and assaulters especially—trumped any desire for privacy. This was the case even for people like Anna, who were partnered.

The secrecy of Anna's jogs related to the taboo nature of running for pleasure and, in particular, the extra calorie consumption it necessitated. For Anna, though, the taboo only added to the feeling of exhilaration that the activity offered. Also, she quelled any guilt with the knowledge that she and her partner were two of the town's most effective salvagers of FAROW (food at risk of wastage).

As Anna neared the town hall and felt a rising wind, something caught her eye on a rose bush growing from a crack in the sidewalk outside the old supermarket. It was half a dozen bright red hips. *And just when I was worrying about my vit-C! . . . How did these get missed by the forager-traders? . . . And how did those thieving birds not get to them first?* She placed the hips into a well used baggie, which she pocketed. The seeds and hairs would be carefully removed later back at the squat. *Actually, screw the vit-C, I might be able to trade these for a few coffee beans.*

At the base of the rose bush, there was a plastic carrier bag from an old electronics store that had been skewered by a large thorn. *Must have blown up the hill from the old woodlot. Shame about that gash.* Could have used it otherwise. Everywhere there were reminders of the squandering by generations past, and the overspend of the energy wealth. The most striking of all these reminders were, for many, the parking lots full of the abandoned electric cars and older vehicles that people once used *just for the sake of it.* These days, HPE (high-power energy) was reserved, on paper, for medical vehicles, sporadic transport of food and water, and the local government's efforts, almost all futile, to keep control. In reality, much of it was used by marauding clans.

Anna reached the entrance to the town hall and passed under a twisting flag bearing the Pokeyhole emblem. On a board inside the doorway she stopped to read a handmade poster promoting a talk that took place, several months back, on the hundred-and-tenth anniversary of the Apollo 11 moon landing. It had been given by some local historian of the collapse. It bore his most quoted saying: "Collapsing societies have a power of hindsight that is simply impossible in growing ones." Next to this poster was another, which advertised the event for which Anna had come, a Thanksgiving session run by the Pokeyhole Positivity Boosters. Times, everyone knew, were bleak. And no matter how much one's skin had thickened, each day threw up the horror of new injustices. Which is why conscious efforts to think positively were felt by many to be a necessary ritual in life.

Anna could see that dozens of people were already there, crowded into the far end of the main hall, away from the damp area under the leaking roof at the near side. As the meeting unfolded, some attendees left, after they'd said their thanks, and more arrived.

Speaking from a dais at the front, as Anna merged into the back of the crowd, was a kind lady, hunched over from years of working the potato fields.

"I'm grateful that Joe's trading his gooseberry wine again this year!"

This expression of gratitude was met with laughter and loud cheers.

The potato digger was followed by octogenarian Isabella Grunter. "I'm grateful that people finally believe me when I said we were having too many children."

"You say that every year," cried a heckler in the middle of the group.

"I know. It's just that I'm still grateful. It was such a mind-boggling taboo for so long."

"Okay, let's not let her get started," retorted the heckler. "Who's next?"

The person next up was one of Pokeyhole's telegram operators. "Logs moving again. Bellows Falls. Winter coming. Need fuel. V grateful."

"We might need fuel," bellowed a different voice, "but the birds need homes!"

"Oh, go and bang your green drum outside, Luis," suggested the heckler. "This meeting's about bleeding positivity, or don't you know what that is?"

Luis was well known in the town as a rare throwback to the conservation movement.

"Everyone gets to be listened to," Luis shouted. "That's the rule."

"That only applies when you're on the stage, Luis! Quick, someone get up there before he does."

Next in the informal queue was an elementary school teacher who was grasping her jaw with her left hand. She said, with some difficulty, "I'm grateful . . . the children persuaded me . . . to get my tooth pulled out. . . . I was in such agony . . . for months . . . but I'm just . . . so squeamish."

She was followed by one of her youngest students, a girl with auburn hair tied in pigtails, whose brief reflection— "I'm grateful for Miss Mosely being so brave"— was greeted with a multitude of appreciative *aww* sounds.

The young girl, in turn, gave way to a man in his early twenties named Billy Sanchez III. "I'm grateful for the magic of baseball. Watching the Pokeyhole Pillagers going twenty-one and five to win the River Championship this year was the best thing in my life so far. And I still can't believe Jesus batted over five hundred. My grandad would have been so proud of them if he was still alive. I don't know what watching big league baseball was like, but there's no way it could have been as good as this."

Anna's turn came soon after and she strode up onto the dais, which was made of five old packaging crates, four placed in a big square as the base and the fifth as a second tier in the middle.

"I'm grateful for the beauty of the night sky . . . and all the thoughts it can help unlock for you. It's the one thing that the previous generation didn't get to enjoy here, with all their—what did they call it?—light pollution."

Anna stepped down carefully and, rather than heading out of the room, as the majority had before her (since the annual event was, for most people, much more about speaking than listening), she decided to return to the back of the group to hear what others had to say.

"Something that I'm ever grateful for is the know-how library by the school. Imagine if no one had bothered to document all those things like tallow candles and natural antiseptics. It would have taken decades to rediscover them. And we all know the salvagers can only do so much."

"I'm grateful for the one good thing Generation Waste left for us, besides stainless steel, which is the national parks. I don't know what we'd have done without all that clean water to drink and all that wood to burn."

Luis bit his tongue, metaphorically, which was still a somewhat painful thing to do to yourself. He estimated that he was about six or eight people away from the front of the group.

"I can build on that one," said the heckler, who had now got his turn on the dais. "I'm grateful for all the carbon dioxide we're putting back in the skies by burning the northern forest. You know, we've got to do something to try and make the winter warmer. It's our civic duty. Nothing less. The one thing I don't understand, though, is why we don't start making CFCs again, to try to knock out the ozone blanket."

And this was what it took for Luis to become enflamed with rage and find himself barging through the front of the assembled group and up onto the platform.

"Right, it's my turn," he yelled, "and you all have to listen. I can't believe what we've done to the forests in the north. And they've still got gasoline up there, can you believe, for running the chainsaws. I've got a friend who canoed down here on the Connecticut and he says there's little left of the trees. Juts big clear-cuts. And we call the previous lot Generation Waste. Well, we're the ones who are burning wood before it even has time to season, which means you have to burn three times as much to get the same heat. And we're still trying to keep cattle rather than using all the fields to grow grain and vegetables for us. It's just such a waste of land. And it's a dream for the looters, because it's a lot easier to take a cow than to pull up a field of carrots. Can no one see how crazy this is!?"

"Okay," interjected the heckler teasingly, "so tell us what you're grateful for, Luis."

"I'm grateful that the collapse is only going to get worse, and wildlife's going to get a chance again because there won't be any people around."

"Right," continued the heckler, with a great satisfaction at Luis having taken his bait. "Let's get this misanthropist under citizen's arrest and down the hill to the jail."

The interruption caused by Luis's outburst and the need for his removal gave those still present a few minutes for quiet reflection. And many of them, including Anna, found themselves thinking that there was some truth in what Luis had said. *They* were still being wasteful. Collapse would, in all likelihood, continue to worsen for a good while. And no one really was able to organize humans in a way that would lift society out of the mire.

Not one person who was yet to speak had anything positive to say any more. Not one of them wanted even to move. And so Anna did something never seen before at this annual gathering. She took to the dais for a second time, twirling a strand of gray hair in front of her eyes as she collected her thoughts.

"Times are tough, yes, but it's no excuse really for the way we're behaving as adults. We are setting a bad example and, the thing is, we're just not going to get any better. . . . I'm grateful for that adorable girl with the pigtails. I'm grateful for her class-mates. . . . Hope lies in the children."

THE LAST ENGLISHMAN

BY CHRISTINE STONE

"HURRY!" BREATHED MEGGY, puffing up the muddy track. "See that cloud?"

The wind was building fast, whipping Henry's shirt sleeves against his thin arms and pushing a strand of grey hair into his eyes. His foot slipped on the wet hillside. This was the fifth—or was it sixth?—hurricane of the season so far and the path up to the refuge cave was the worse for wear. Clutching a basket of precious pans and knives, he caught up with her just as they came over the ledge.

"If you didn't pack so much stuff we wouldn't be so late," he muttered, only half intending her to hear. They had made two trips already, having realised some hours ago what was coming. You learnt to read the wind and waves from a young age on this island.

"If I didn't pack so much stuff, you wouldn't have the benefit of my cooking." Her eyes were not so young these days, but there was nothing wrong with her ears.

The first drops of rain fell. "Get in here will you," Tanno shouted against the noise of excited chatter and billowing palm trees. "We need to get the door up."

Henry could see dozens of the islanders in the half-light inside the cave, possessions piled up around them. Everyone knew the routine; soon they all settled in for the night, glad that they were not on farm duty in one of the caves set aside for the animals. Henry and Meggy sat on cushions and shared a warm blanket over their shoulders. Glass portholes, inches deep, let in a bit of light and they could make out the shapes of friends and neighbours. Someone played a wooden flute and several voices joined in a rousing song.

Like the many other storm-shelter caves in the hills, this one was dry and safe. It was partly natural, partly man-made, with a thick concrete extension around the opening making a kind of hall. The caves had been dug out by the forebears in the Bright Age, to cope with the ever more frequent hurricanes.

It was dawn the next day when the rain stopped. Meggy and Henry were among the first out, being nearer the door. The sun lit up the Eastern horizon below a bank of blue-grey cloud and the wind was dying down. They seemed to have got off lightly this time. Meggy hurried off to find which cave her grandchildren were in.

"Hey, Henry, there's someone I'd like you to meet."

Henry turned to see young Tanno Galvez, his sister's nephew-in-law, with a pale-looking stranger.

"This is Mr. Marcano, he's from the mainland. Meet Henry Tilbury, our Curator." Tanno was a bright and lively twenty-year-old, with his mother's grace and manners.

"Please, call me Felipe," said Mr. Marcano, holding his hand up, fingers slightly splayed and palm forward. "Oh sorry, habit." He lowered his hand to grasp Henry's. "I'm still getting used to the way you shake hands around here." His accent was strong, making it hard to catch what he was saying.

"Pleased to meet you," said Henry, wondering who this stranger was.

"Felipe just arrived yesterday morning," said Tanno. "I saw him down at the dock and brought him up here for the night."

"Is your boat safe?" enquired Henry politely. The man looked way too smartly dressed for a fisherman.

"I hope so, although it wasn't my boat—I'm no sailor. A ferryship brought me from Kitts. The crew took advice about the storm and went to shelter with some fishermen. You are lucky to have these caves for shelter."

"Yeah, well, I guess without them we wouldn't stand much of a chance. Don't you get hurricanes where you live?

"Not often. Shall we go on down to the harbour and I'll explain why I am here?" Felipe suggested.

Half an hour later, they were sitting on upturned logs, sipping bark tea, while all around them the islanders were checking on the damage and catching up with neighbours. Some were already heaving the specially rounded storm stones off the wooden wall panels of their huts and starting to reassemble the simple dwellings. The hardwood shingled roofs would take a bit longer to resurrect, but at least walls gave the illusion of privacy and demarcated boundaries.

"So let me get this straight," said Henry. "You want to take the Heritage back to Zwayla and put it in a museum?"

"No, not exactly a museum, Henry—to the Versity of Cracas. We just want to assess the condition of the artefacts, you understand? To see what preservation is needed. So little is left from the Bright Age, and more is being lost all the time. We hear that your collection is sizeable? The very best care would be taken of it, of course."

"Well, I'm not so sure about that. I don't hear you talking about a loan or bringing it back." Felipe started to speak again, but Henry carried on, "No, you listen to me! Our Heritage belongs right here on this island. It doesn't need any preserving. It is perfectly safe. And it doesn't need studying either. I know where it all came from, how it was passed down. We all know what the Heritage means to us."

"But surely, if I could just make an initial assessment, I could . . ."

"No!" said Henry, a little more loudly than he intended. "No, I'm sorry but the answer is no."

"Well now," Tanno chipped in, "let's not be hasty. I'm sure the council will want to consider the matter."

"No need. I'm the Curator. The Heritage is my sole responsibility—you know that." His annoyance fuelled a proud grandiosity. He turned back to Marcano. "The last Governor of these British Virgin Islands left the Heritage collection to be kept by the Curator, in the name of Queen Charlotte the second of England and her heirs. I'm the fifth Curator in line. My great-great grandfather was entrusted to keep the Heritage safe. We need it. It shows us where we came from and keeps us from forgetting who we are. We are British, English." He paused, looking around the little settlement. Neither Felipe nor Tanno spoke. "You know," he continued gently, "lots of people come and go, looking for fish, or wood, or some place to settle. Gyanans, Zillians, Zwaylans, Mexies, even Mercans make it out here sometimes. Sometimes they talk in a speech we can understand, sometimes not. We trade what we can. Most don't cause trouble. But we stay. We are English, and this is our island. It is what makes us who we are, a people, not wandering souls. This Heritage came down to us from England. It is not going to Zwayla, not now, not ever." Another pause. He stood up. "Now, if you'll excuse me, I've got a house to rebuild."

The United Kingdom of Great Britain and Northern Ireland, to give it its full name, had lasted little over a century. Northern Ireland was the first part to go, cut adrift when Britain turned its back on the European Union like a penguin abandoning a doomed iceberg. It suffered a kind of quasi-independence for a while before resignedly re-uniting with the rest of Ireland. Of course, the Scots soon voted for their independence. As the Bright Age slid into its long decline, bits and pieces of the old heartland of empire were given freedom, or cut themselves loose, or simply got lost along the way. Wales absorbed much of the land out to the shell of Birmingham, Offa's Dyke no longer forming the ancient border but becoming the backbone of the resurgent Celtic nation. Northumberland threw its lot in with the Scots; Hadrian's Wall was the new boundary, Rome casting its long shadow down the millennia. Cornwall gained a long-dreamt-of independence and then joined with Devon, Dorset, and Somerset to become West Britain. Hampshire and Wiltshire renamed themselves the Republic of Wessex. London had long seen which way the wind was blowing; it shook off the moribund inland areas and declared itself an independent city state. Monopolising the mouth of the Thames, it prospered as a sea port, adapting to the rising seas by creeping inland; old buildings were abandoned to the waves and new ones thrown up further inland. Liverpool and Newcastle followed suit.

As The Chaos drew in, distances lengthened and good fertile land became scarcer. What was left of England fell into the usual dukedoms and warzones. Over the centuries somehow the very word "England" fell out of use and was left to the history books.

The Crown Dependencies or Overseas Territories fared mixed fates. The populations of the most remote islands, frightened by precarious supply lines and rising seas, abandoned them to the birds and mammalian invaders. Natural selection took its course. Argentina claimed the Falklands, but those islands were too far from the mainland to be held in any kind of firm grip. Brittany and Normandy split the Channel Islands between them.

And out in the Caribbean, the British Virgin Islands were forgotten.

Later that morning, Tanno and Felipe were leading two pigs on ropes down a wide path from one of the animal storm caves. The pigs belonged to Tanno's father, on whose farm the young man worked. To Felipe's credit, he did not object to lending a hand with the many tasks that needed doing after the storm. He seemed interested in every aspect of life on the island.

Tanno was equally interested in Felipe. "So, how did you know to come here? How did you know about our Heritage?"

"Traders and fishermen travel up and down all along the island chain, as far down to the mainland, and they do like to talk. The Versity has for many years now been sending out expeditionary scouts who listen and follow leads. It is our main project to gather up what we can that is left from the Bright Age. So much has been lost."

"So you're a scout?"

"No, I'm a field researcher. We come in after a lead has been confirmed, and send back what we find to the Versity for the professors to study. Tell me about this Heritage of yours. I understand the artefacts are in a cave?"

"Oh yes, the Heritage Cave. We use it for ceremonies. I had my majority ceremony there a couple of summer's ago."

"That's interesting. I'd really like to see it."

"I expect the council will consider it. We don't normally take outsiders, but I can't see the harm in you having a look." Tanno changed the subject to what really interested him. "So if you're a field researcher, have you been to lots of places?"

"Quite a few. I've been all down the coast of Gyana to Brazil, and lots of islands."

"Isn't it scary travelling alone? I mean, how do you talk to people and see if they're friendly?

"Oh I'm not always alone; sometimes I have a research partner. But most people are friendly if you know how to approach them. The Zillians are a bit more difficult; their language comes from Portogeese, so it's harder to be understood there."

"Where else have you been?" asked Tanno, eager to hear more.

"Pertorico, Iyspanola, lots of places. Clumbia. I saw Panama too. That was amazing".

Tanno's eyes opened wide. "Did the forebears really dig a river all the way to the other side, to the other ocean?"

"Oh yes, it's quite a sight. It's called a canal. There's different sections going all through the hills and joining the lakes. Lord knows how they did it."

"I want to travel. I want to get off this stupid island. All I do is mind dumb animals and scratch a living in the dirt. I want to go places and wear nice clothes like you."

Felipe grinned. "Zwayla's a wealthy country, and I have a good job. You could go there and do well—there's lots of opportunities."

"That would be so great. Can I go back with you?"

"Err, well, sure. If you're serious. It depends how my trip here works out. Maybe you can help me with this council. I said Zwayla was wealthy; what kind of thing would the council like as a gift?"

"A gift?" Tanno was taken aback, then thought for a moment. "Wood," he said. "Building wood—we always need strong building wood and it's not easy to trade for it."

"Great, I'm sure that can be arranged." Felipe was relieved it would be so easy. "Zwayla has lots of forests now. They were protected by the forebears, so in The Chaos nobody dared touch them out of superstition. When can you introduce me to the council?"

Henry slept badly that night. He woke stiff and despondent. The sun was already high in the sky. Meggy, bless her, had coffee and panbread ready. She looked at him sideways from a yoga stretch.

"Hate to tell you," she said, straightening up, "but Tanno and that Mr. Felipe have already been to see chairman Gella. They want you over at the council—sent a young lad with a message just a minute ago." She bent in the other direction and nodded to the table where a small polished wooden slate lay. Henry took it and read the scratchy charcoaled note while gulping still-warm coffee.

"What's Tanno doing meddling in this?" he growled. "He's not on the council. He's got no business sticking his oar in."

"I guess he just likes being helpful. Felipe is staying with him."

"Well, I better go and put a stop to this nonsense." He pulled on his trousers and tunic.

"Mind how you go barging in there", frowned Meggy, stretching her arms up and arching backwards. "The council won't take kindly to you getting all steamed up."

"Never mind about me." He picked up a slab of bread, planted a kiss on her cheek and strode off.

The council hall hadn't yet been put back together, so they were all sitting on rocks and wooden benches. A quick glance told him Tanno and Felipe Marcano weren't there. There were twelve members, elected every five years, including Chairman Gella. She was a young widow, her husband having died at sea a few years ago. He had left her well off; she was the owner of two good boats that she rented out, and a good bit of land that her sister's family farmed.

"Good morning," she called, seeing Henry approach. "Thank you for coming. I trust you and Meggy came through alright?"

"Fine, thanks. Meggy is fine. So what is this all about? You know I am Curator."

"Well, okay, let's get straight to the point then."

The meeting went on for over an hour. Some councillors sided with Henry and tried to close down the debate on the grounds that the Council had no jurisdiction over the Curator or the Heritage. Gella disagreed. Some were in favour of letting Felipe Marcano take the Heritage on a loan for study. Someone suggested it could be studied on the island, but Felipe disagreed; he needed special equipment only available at the Versity. He put forward the offer of a large shipment of good building hardwood in exchange for the loan of the artefacts. A few councillors were persuaded by the offer, which caused quite a shouting match until Gella settled them all down with the threat of de-selection from their seats. After the arguments had gone round in circles at least three times, she called a halt.

"We are all agreed that these are valuable items, precious to our people. They have been passed down a long line of Governors and Curators. But I think perhaps the time has come to look at them with a fresh perspective. I suggest we meet tomorrow afternoon, when tempers have had a chance to cool, and all go up to the

Heritage Cave to re-connect with the items before considering our next steps. I for one have not actually looked at them since my wedding ceremony years ago. The meeting is adjourned."

"How did it go?" enquired Meggy, pushing aside the vine curtain in the doorway of their hut as he approached.

"They're not listening to me. Gella says they'll all go up to the Heritage cave tomorrow and take a look before they decide."

"Are you going with them?"

"I don't know. I'll think about it." He saw the digging stick in her hand. "Were you just starting on the garden?"

"Yes, want to join me?"

"Yeah, I'll check how the potatoes are doing."

They spent a pleasant few hours rescuing and restoring the vegetable patch. Before the storm they had deliberately buried some of the smaller plants up to their top leaves to save them from the wind, but had not had time to do them all. The trailing beans had been carefully laid flat and covered in a thin layer of earth; they now needed re-tying to their poles. All-in-all, the damage was about as expected.

Later, Meggy looked up to see Gella coming along the dirt track. "Hi, Henry has just gone to Mike's to borrow a metal spade. He won't be long."

"It's you I've come to see," smiled Gella. "How did the garden come through?"

"Not too bad. We've lost some of the corn, but most of the plants are okay. How can I help?"

"I guess Henry has filled you in on the meeting this morning?"

"A bit. Shall we sit?"

They sat on the warm ground and Gella recounted the morning's discussion. She summed up the situation: "So, Mr. Marcano has offered a shipment of hardwood if we let him borrow the Heritage. I think we should take the offer."

"I don't know," Meggy sighed. She thought for a moment. "I feel we should keep it; the Heritage is a big part of our tradition." She paused. "Then again, Henry isn't getting any younger, and you know he has no children of his own. Who will be Curator after him? My grandchildren aren't interested."

Gella nodded in agreement. "We could make the council responsible for the Heritage if there are no more Curators, but votes can change from one year to the next. I don't think it would be secure in the long term. Already some want to let it go to the mainland, and we could really do with the wood." She gazed out over the village below them, to the harbour and the open sea beyond. Most of the small homes were now standing again, and some already had their roofs. But there was no denying how tatty and worn it all looked. Some of the boats had suffered real damage, including one of hers. She had always tried to do the right thing being on the council, but it wasn't straightforward. There was no doubt they needed wood, but was that need really more important than the Heritage?

"The thing is," pondered Meggy, as if answering Gella's unspoken thoughts, "young people just don't see the relevance. I talk to the mums and youngsters—nobody much cares. They don't feel the connection to their history. Maybe we need to keep the Heritage and make it relevant again. We can't lose sight of our past. If we don't know where we came from, how can we go forward? The Heritage is what keeps us together."

Gella paused to consider this. "No," she said slowly, "I don't think that's right. What keeps us together is family. The island. We all look out for each other. Practically everyone is related to someone." As she talked, her thoughts and feelings became clearer. She was a practical, unsentimental woman, not given to prioritising the abstract over the tangible. "I don't think a collection of Heritage helps us. And if we don't let it go to the mainland now, we may not get another chance. Besides, maybe it really would be better cared for in the Versity."

The firmness of Gella's voice was persuasive. Meggy was not afraid to argue with anyone when needed, but perhaps Gella was right on this. She turned her head and glanced back at their hut. It was cosy and tidy inside, but the repeated dismantling over the years was certainly taking its toll. "I guess we really do need the wood. I don't fancy a roof of leaves instead of shingles. So many of them are cracked now —they won't last."

Gella was relieved. Meggy's change of heart seemed to confirm her own inclinations. Hopefully the meeting tomorrow would settle the matter. "Will you and Henry both come to the cave tomorrow? I am asking several elders to come and let us know their thoughts."

"Sure, we'll be there."

Felipe was watching Tanno milk one of the goats when he looked up and saw Gella approaching. He had met her briefly before the meeting that morning, and had spent most of the day wondering how it went, but he was too experienced in fieldwork to hurry the process and risk causing offence.

"Hello again, Mr. Marcano."

"Please, call me Felipe."

"Hello Felipe. Hello Tanno. Is your father around?"

"He's down at the harbour with Grandad. Can I help?"

"No, thanks. I'm going that way next." She turned to Felipe. "I'm sorry to keep you waiting. The council haven't reached a decision yet but we are meeting again tomorrow." She smiled. "I'm sure the council can be persuaded. It is a very generous offer you have made. I will come and see you tomorrow as soon as we have decided." With a wide smile, she turned and walked back over the field.

After she was out of earshot, Tanno turned eagerly to Felipe. "If she's on our side, it will be okay."

"Let's hope so."

"We'll be on our way back to Zwayla before you know it!"

Felipe didn't reply, but fixed a smile on his face.

Early next morning, Henry was up before Meggy stirred. He sat mulling over recent events. Finally, he decided not to wait until the afternoon; he would go and move as much as he could out of the cave and hide it somewhere until that wretched Felipe Marcano had gone back to Zwayla. He was soon up and out.

It was not often that even he made the pilgrimage to the Heritage Cave. It was one of the highest, up a rocky slope that was not well-trodden. Traditionally, majorities, baby-namings and weddings were held on the plateau in front of the cave, with a magnificent view out over the whole island. But the last couple of weddings had been held down near the harbour, on a beach right next to the sea. Young people today had no idea what was right and proper.

Eventually, he reached the beautifully fitted oak door, sealed to keep out all moisture, and took out a large brass key from his bag. Already his resolve was wavering, the long walk in the early sunshine having dissipated his bad mood. Where on earth could he take the things? He couldn't save the Heritage all by himself. He had no idea what to do.

Inside, he looked around the cave, sunlight pouring in the open door, and saw it as if with new eyes. Only the low rock roof betrayed the location, for the walls were all panelled with waxed wood and lined with glass-doored cases. A thick carpet of some old Bright Age material covered the levelled floor, defying the best efforts of time. But for the slight mustiness of the air and the sounds of tropical birds behind him, he could have been in a fine drawing room in a Governor's house, just like his dad had described in the Curator Stories when he was a boy.

The cases were full: books, vases, sculptures, small paintings, ornaments, carved boxes of trinkets and oddments, yet more books, small metal machines and tools of all kinds, some with uses long forgotten. In one case, a metal pen, which must have had internal ink long ago, balanced on a pile of disintegrating papers. There was a ball on a tall stand showing the whole world as it used to be. Henry turned it and marvelled at the sight of all the Caribbean islands that had long since disappeared beneath the waves.

It struck him: these were relics of a civilisation long gone. What relevance did they have to their lives now? Even when people came here for the ceremonies and rituals, no one looked too closely inside the cave. They stayed mostly out on the plateau in the warm sun for the speeches, before heading back down to the celebrations, to where life happened.

Trembling slightly, he opened one of the glass cases and took down an ancient leather-bound volume. He wondered how many decades, perhaps even centuries, it had been since the book was last opened. He placed it on the central table and opened it gingerly, supporting one side to take the stress off the brittle spine. Mould had crept in behind the glass of the case and was feasting on the edges of the decaying paper. Henry stared at the page. The black inked letters had faded and smudged in places, but they were mostly clear enough. Some of the letters had strange shapes, quite unlike those he had learned as a boy. Some he recognised, but others had the wrong tails or stalks, or were bent this way or that. He could only make sense of about one word in three. Slowly, Henry George Tilbury, the last Englishman, realised that he neither read, nor spoke, English.

THE WIZARD-KINGS OF YUSAI

BY DAVID ENGLAND

"CAN YOU TELL US A STORY, GRANDPA?"

I glanced up from the small flame I was carefully nursing to life with twigs and kindling. The bright eyes of the younger of my son's two boys examined me through the thin column of smoke with a disconcerting intensity. My reservations about this outing resurfaced with a vengeance, but I pushed them aside with equal vigor.

"In a short while, Jude," I replied with a seeming casualness, returning my attention to the infant fire in an effort to mask the rising apprehension in my heart. "Let's finish setting up camp before we get to the story-telling. Why don't you help your brother gather some firewood? We'll need more for tonight and the morning yet."

The boy nodded in that familiar, too-adult way that belied his mere six summers and looked over to his older brother. Two years Jude's senior, Micah was the undisputed leader of the pair and responded with a curt nod of his own.

"Come on, Jude. I'll show you what to look for. Just like Pa showed me."

I kept my focus on the growing fire, keeping the apprehension clenching my gut from revealing itself in my expression. This life is a harsh and unrelenting tutor, I reminded myself. The gods do not coddle us, having learned that lesson at some expense in their dealings with our ancient ancestors. Such is the way of this world.

Simon had been a good man, a fine husband and father. Certainly, my Hattie and I could not have asked for a better son. But the gods are a fickle lot, freely mixing blessings with cursings, giving with one hand while taking away with the other.

The fire burned strongly now, having been built up with ever-larger sticks. I added several lengths of logs to give it a solid fuel supply and moved over to where our birch bark canoe was pulled up onto the shore. A line fastened to the stern trailed into the water, our day's catch secured at the far end. The boys had hunted well, having brought in several large fish with their short, darting spear-thrusts. I drew the fish in, pulled my knife from its sheath on my hip, and began to prepare our food for the fire.

Simon had been the only child the gods had seen fit to bestow upon Hattie and me, closing her womb in the wake of his difficult birth. Even then, it would seem, the seed of the wasting disease that would take her from me lay sleeping in her belly. But that sorrow was still many years in the future at Simon's birth and in the intervening years, he grew strong and tall with all the vigor of youth.

Our farm lay outside the village, at a distance but not so far as to be remote. We travelled into town with some frequency and always took part in the festivals and holy rites. Mostly, though, we tilled our land, cultivating crops for food and trade. We kept chickens, of course, and a few dairy goats, but ours was a crop farm, not an animal farm, and our energies were focused on the corn and beans and root vegetables we supplied to the local markets.

I remember how I felt my chest might have burst with pride that morning at breakfast when Simon announced to our astonishment that he had found himself a wife. It had been only early summer, not that far removed from the Spring Rites during which he'd gone through the initiation from child to adult, alongside the other of the surrounding region who'd attained the age of fifteen. Seems that he'd been putting his plans in place all that previous winter and, when afforded the opportunity by an errand-run into town, had marched himself right up to Rebecca Atkins, the seamstress' apprentice, and asked her if she would be willing to be bound with him.

Their union was witnessed prior to the Summer Rite and Micah came along nine moons later. Hattie was overjoyed, as the disease was beginning to make itself known by that point. At least she had been able to see Jude born into the world two years later before she closed her eyes for the last time.

"We're back, Grandpa!" Micah announced as he and Jude emerged from the trees, each bearing an armload of wood.

"Very good, boys," I replied and waved to the file of firewood I'd gathered earlier. "Add those to our stack and come help me get these fish cooking."

Moving with the energy exhibited by youth whenever food is involved, the two of them quickly deposited their burdens and gathered to me by the fire. Together, we wove the utensils with which to hold the fish from green limbs, staking them into the ground at an angle over the fire. Soon, the aroma of the anticipated meal filled our nostrils. We rotated the fish once to help them cook more evenly, but a short time later our meals were cooling on flat rocks as we prepared to eat.

"Can you tell us a story *now?*" Jude asked with impatience.

"Jude," Micah admonished his sibling. "Grandpa will tell us a story when he is good and ready." The younger boy frowned and turned his attention to the steaming, flaky meat of the whitefish.

The shadow of my fears loomed in the darkening air around us as night descended and I briefly considered side-stepping the talk I'd intended the three of us to have. But then Rebecca's face appeared in my thoughts, her eyes like the open sky on a cloudless day, and I heard her soft voice as she said again in my memory the words she'd spoken to me privately in the days before the boys and I had departed.

"Jerome," she'd said quietly. "I know your fears. But this needs be done." Her hand had gone to her belly, even now beginning to round with life. "Time grows short."

I looked at the boys across the flames. The two of them could not be more different. Micah was the very image of his father, with Simon's hazel eyes and thick, brown hair the color of rich soil. Jude, on the other hand, reflected their mother: ash-blond locks, a light dusting of freckles, and bright blue eyes. I took a deep breath and exhaled slowly.

"A story, then."

The boys said nothing, but leaned in with obvious interest as they continued to devour the fish.

"Far to the east lay the Great Ocean," I said. "Now, this Ocean is vast and deep, far bigger than even the Shygan." The boys' eyes went wide, as they'd both been to the shore of the big water at the end of the river and I could see them trying to imagine something even more vast. "The Ocean has something else, too," I continued. "Its waters are filled with salt, unlike those of the Shygan, and traders from the east bring this salt with them in their caravans for trade with us here." I saw Micah nod and smiled. He'd been helping his mother with breadmaking for some months now and knew how precious those pinches of white crystals were to the process.

"But the Great Ocean hasn't always been where it is today," I told them. "Long, long ago, when our ancient ancestors walked the earth, the Great Ocean lay much further to the east and lands that are now far beneath the waves once felt the caresses of the winds and saw the light of the sun.

"In those ancient times arose the vast kingdom of Yusai. This kingdom was ruled by powerful wizard-kings who dwelt in two cities perched on the shores of the Great Ocean. These were the legendary cities of Nor and D'Say . . ."

The wizard-kings of Nor were sorcerers of gold, with the power to create precious metals and gems from the very air. They built tall towers that reached up to touch the very sky and they dwelt in these towers among the clouds, casting their spells and gathering their wealth.

The wizard-kings of D'Say, on the other hand, were sorcerers of men. They commanded uncountable legions and vast armies of metal servants that crawled over the land and flew through the air and swam in the waters. They dwelt in sprawling halls of marble, casting their spells and commanding their forces. And for many years, the wizard-kings of the two cities ruled over Yusai, and even lands beyond.

At first, the wizard-kings were content with their domains, but over the generations, they became lustful of other lands and greedy for more wealth, more power. Those of Nor sought to add to their already-bountiful hoards and those of D'Say sought to extend their influence. Together, the two cities decided that they must extend their rule to the entirety of the world.

And so, the wizard-kings reached into the dark depths of their arcane arts, calling upon powers to which no human had any right. They brought forth these powers from the realms of shadow and with their aid they did indeed enlarge the domains of Yusai to all lands beneath the sun.

For generations afterward, the wizard-kings held sway over all the earth, the winds of the sky, and the waters of Ocean. All that walked or swam or flew paid homage to Nor and D'Say.

But the powers which the sorcerers had summoned to do their bidding exacted a terrible price. The very cosmos turned against the rulers of the cities as the gods themselves grew weary of the wizard-kings' insolence. The lands were made parched and dry, denying the people sustenance. The earth shook, toppling vast cities. From the skies, storms raged. The very waters of the Ocean began to rise.

The nations of the earth became vexed with the rule of the wizard-kings of Yusai. Long had the sorcerers' greed and arrogance been tolerated, for the rule of Nor and D'Say had quelled war among the peoples, allowing for trade and prosperity. But as the wizard-kings took more wealth for themselves, less was left for the nations, who began to murmur against the wizard-kings.

But the sorcerers in their cloud towers and their marble halls scoffed at the nations of the earth, confident in the supreme power of their sorcery. Those nations who rebelled were crushed without mercy as a warning to others. Yet the gods continued to raise the elements of the cosmos against Nor and D'Say. And in their foolish pride, the wizard-kings scoffed at even the gods.

So the gods freed the arcane powers summoned by the wizard-kings, unleashing them from their bonds, and the powers turned against the rulers of Yusai. The storms raged more powerfully, the lands shook in great anger, and the waters of the Oceans swallowed the shores. The nations revolted against the sorcerers of the two cities, overthrowing their cloud-towers and marble halls. And when this was done, the peoples of the earth called upon the gods for mercy, as the kingdom of Yusai and the arrogance of its wizard-kings were no more.

The gods heard the cries of the peoples and relented in their divine anger, but not before the Ocean had overrun the shores where the legendary cities had once stood, now forever lost beneath the waves as a lesson to men.

‡‡

"... and this is why we honor the gods in the Rites of the Seasons, why we live on this land with humility. The gods taught the peoples of the earth a harsh lesson and to this day we bear the burdens of that lesson." I looked at each of the boys in turn. "It is very important that we remember the cost of arrogance and the price of power, that we remember the lessons of the prideful wizard-kings of Yusai."

I fell silent. Micah and Jude stared at me over the low fire, their mouths slightly open and the cooling whitefish momentarily forgotten. Nodding to myself, I felt a warm glow of pride--if nothing else, I can still tell a good story. I allowed another moment to savor the magic and then broke the spell, gesturing to the boys' food.

The two youths blinked, as if coming from a trance, and then dove into the fish, ravenous in a way I recalled all-too-well from my own childhood. We must relish these times, I reminded myself, for life takes them from us far too quickly. Chewing my own food in thoughtful silence, I worked up my nerve to broach the next, needed topic.

I cleared my throat. "There is something else we need to talk about, boys."

Micah and Jude exchanged glances. Micah looked at me with a level gaze and spoke in that all-too-adult manner. "You're gonna replace Pa." It was a statement, not a question. My eyes jumped to Jude, who said nothing, then back to his older brother.

"Who told you that, Micah?" I asked, trying to display a confidence I didn't feel. Rebecca and I were pushing the bounds of tradition as it was. But nothing would work if the boys rebelled.

"No one," Micah responded. "Jude and I see things, though." His eyes considered me carefully. "You and Ma look at each other the same way she and Pa did before he died."

Before the winter hunt he didn't return from. Before the spring thaw when we'd found his body beneath the broken ice of the lake. Before these boys had lost their father, Rebecca had lost her husband, and I had lost my son.

The gods give and the gods take away.

Neither of us had meant for what had happened to happen. Rebecca was finding her way as a young widow and our household had adjusted to one less person. I worked our fields, taught the boys what I could this last summer, and went about mourning my own losses. A common enough tale in this age. But the gods had other plans. Not that Rebecca and I didn't contribute in our own manner, certainly.

It had been the time of the Summer Rites. We'd ridden back to our homestead from the village on that longest day of the year. The boys had fallen asleep and we'd put them to bed as the shadows of evening started to descend. But the rites had brought fire to our blood. An energy crackled between Rebecca and I that had been lying in wait, patient and quiet, for many months. I'd fought my own urges and went about the evening as normally as I could, but my eyes had lingered on her form while my thoughts caressed her lean curves.

I'd gone to bed in my room, the last of the sunlight dwindling away on the other side of the window, when my door opened and Rebecca entered. Her eyes burned into me and without a word, she pulled her robe away and let it fall to the floor, leaving her clothed only in the gathering shadows. I stepped to her, pulled her body to mine, and we took one another.

And now it was time to face up to what we had done, for the gods had gifted us with a child that night.

There was no way but through.

"Yes," I nodded to the boys. "It is true. Your mother and I intend to be bound. You will have a brother or a sister in another half-year's time." I swallowed, pushing down my insecurity. "How do you two feel about that?"

"You can't be our Pa," Jude blurted out. My heart sank.

Micah elbowed his brother. "Jude and I have talked about it," he said. "We won't let Pa be forgot. You can't be Pa." He looked at me carefully. "But you are Pa's father, so we decided that we can call you Papa instead."

And with those words, as powerful an incantation as any ancient sorcery, all my doubts, all the shadow demons which had haunted my heart for these past weeks and months were banished. The wizard-kings of Yousai have nothing over these boys, I thought. Nothing at all.

"I would like that very much," I replied.

ALL THAT GLITTERS

BY JEANNE LABONTE

DOCTOR ABRAM DUBOIS READIED HIS PLIERS FOR ANOTHER PULL. The dog rolled his eyes at the sight of the pliers but otherwise made no protest other than uttering a small yip of pain as each quill was extracted. It helped that the dog's owner, a farmer with the impressive name of Tomaz Jefferson Franklin Lorenzo, held the dog's body firmly in place with his muscular legs, his big calloused hands gripping the collar. There was no escape.

"Ordinarily I pull them out myself," said the Ginian farmer, his rough gravelly voice emanating from somewhere deep inside his reddish-brown beard. "He usually gets just a little snoot-full, but this time—"

"*Yip!*"

"No, you were right to bring him in," replied Abram, examining the quill he had just pulled to make sure it was intact. "Some of those quills were dangerously close to his eyes. Looks like the porcupine got lucky and swatted him right across the face."

"Well, he won't do that again!" declared Tomaz. "He's porcupine soup tonight!"

"*Yip!*"

"Well, with any luck Roller here will have a bite of it," said the Essene, a wry smile appearing on his bearded face. "Maybe get a little revenge."

The Ginian farmer laughed. It had been an otherwise quiet morning at the small hospital. Earlier Abram had treated a poison ivy rash on an incautious young boy. His mother had first daubed the boy's rash with a reeking ointment she had obtained from an herbalist in the city, but after it produced a rash of its own both on her child and herself, she brought the lad to Abram, complaining furiously about the old fraud who sold it to her. Abram knew the man and his questionable nostrums. It wasn't the first time he had to undo damage caused by some old half-remembered remedy. It was easy to see why the physicians of Richmound, capital of the small Ginia Republic, had written to him on hearing of his presence in the New Bostonia Commonwealth. While most local rural people utilized their own tried and true cures, the slowly expanding population of the city was creating a demand for ready-made medicines, a situation encouraging quacks and ill-educated physickers to step forward and try filling the gap. The need for some sort of organized medical system was growing.

"*Yip!*"

"Have courage, my friend," chuckled Abram, dropping another quill into the bowl, the pile growing impressively large. "We're almost done. I just wish my teachers could see me doing this."

"How do you mean?" asked Tomaz.

"Well, in my homeland across the sea, the Essene order only treats people. Animals are either treated by their owners or by people called veterinaria. I don't think it ever occurred to anyone to combine the two the way you have done here."

"*Yip!*"

"Well then, sir, you must have got quite a shock when you first came here," laughed the farmer.

"That I did." Abram chuckled again, recalling his initial dismay on discovering his first patient on the North American continent was a cow with an infected udder. "But I learned to adapt."

"*Yip!*"

"And that, my brave hero, is the last one," said Abram, looking down in satisfaction at the now quill-free dog.

"Until the next time," said Tomaz dryly. "He never seems to learn, that one. We treasure our animals here. It just wouldn't be possible to survive without them. Why wouldn't we treat them as our brethren? I've heard of people misusing their animals, but that's just risking the wrath of the Saints. Ravael would no longer protect them against sickness, Arzula would close up the wombs of their women, Appleseed would leave the fields and trees barren!" The farmer shook his head as he caressed Roller, who seemed grateful his ordeal was over.

For payment Tomaz left a basket of fresh eggs. Country folk making use of the little hospital Abram had helped set up just outside Richmound invariably paid with produce, tobacco and other goods. Only the city people paid with the small aluminum or silver coins minted in Richmound. He had no personal use for the coins because of his Essene vows of simplicity, using them instead to purchase supplies for the hospital. Any unneeded goods he received, such as baskets, pottery or shoes, he donated to the local shrines for distribution to the needy.

The hospital was small compared to the larger establishments in the Commonwealths to the north and the Essene hospitals back home. Chaos over the centuries had been the rule here, from incessant warfare following the collapse of the old government a millennium before to diasporas from Central America and the Caribbean, as well as climatic gyrations and epidemics. A massive earthquake deep inland in the twenty-sixth century, followed two centuries later by a devastating tsunami along the southern coastlines, thought to have originated from a volcanic explosion in the Caribbean, all conspired to keep this part of North America badly fragmented and far less sophisticated than the two Commonwealths and First People Nation far to the north.

But the land and the people were resilient. The current Ginia Republic, the latest in a series, seemed to be taking lasting root. Abram surveyed the four-room hospital, now quiet, with the twelve-bed sick area empty of patients. A warm but refreshing breeze fluttered the single remaining veil of mosquito netting over one of the beds. Mid-morning sunshine brightened the examining room as he checked the cupboards to ensure supplies were on hand. Consuela must have been here earlier because the tiny metal wood stove had a pot of broth heating.

Five others hospitals were in the city itself, the product of the combined efforts of Abram, the local physicians, and the numerous religious groups which formed a colorful quilt of sacred beliefs. Abram recognized the origins of a few, such as the Society of God's Children, an ancient Protestant sect, and the Church of the Holy Mother, a distant offshoot of the Old Catholic church, while others like the Pathways of the Saints, the predominating religion, seemed far more obscure, possibly a mix of Christianity and the plethora of odd pagan sects that cropped up during the Terrible Ages. Abram wished he could delve more into the local histories, but never quite seemed to have the time.

A noise outside the door made him look up.

"Oh, shoo, you silly cat. I'll fall over you if you keep rubbing my legs like that!" Consuela stepped into the examining room, her round, brown arms clutching a tall stack of folded mosquito netting. A small ginger cat kept coiling about her legs and mewing, perhaps in hopes of a snack.

"Here, let me take that," laughed Abram, taking the netting from the stout middle-aged midwife.

"Wherever did that creature come from?"

"Miguel brought him. He assured me the cat's a good mouser but the little fellow seems more interested in colonizing people's laps."

"If Miguel was the one who brought him, that cat's probably spoiled rotten. But I'm sure he'll earn his keep eventually." The midwife sat down on a bench, wiping the perspiration from her square plain face. "I wish that Christos refugee camp wasn't so close. I still think it was they who stole the netting we had here before."

"Possibly. But since no one saw anything, I think it would be better to give them the benefit of the doubt. They haven't troubled anyone and keep mostly to themselves," replied Abram, who secretly agreed with her but was mindful of his mentors' teachings not to pass judgment.

The winter before last, the Christos had fought with the New York Commonwealth and suffered a devastating defeat, their leader killed. As a result, civil strife erupted in the insular little country, sandwiched between the Commonwealths and the Ginia Republic, as various clans fought to fill the vacuum left. Refugees, mostly farmers, fled both north and south to escape the violence. Unfortunately, thanks to the rigid form of old Christianity they clung to, they refused to enter any villages or towns of the "devil worshipers" they had been taught to loathe, staying instead in little camps. Some had begun accepting food offered to them but otherwise made no effort to interact with any of the local people. Abram found it hard not to look at them with a jaundiced eye, mindful of the story the Palachian woman Nahomi had told him of her harrowing upbringing among them.

Still, he wished there was some way to break the ice. Early each morning, he passed by the encampment situated on the other side of the stream running near the hospital. Peering through the trees, he could see people cooking and doing small chores. The sound of a cow wanting to be milked emanated from somewhere in the camp. Several women busied themselves weaving with hand spindles in front of make-shift tents and he often spotted children hiding in the brush watching him as he walked by. Today, though, he had seen no children running about playing. Had something happened? Sickness was a real possibility with the likely squalid conditions of the camp and the recent hot weather they had been experiencing. Given their xenophobia, however, any uninvited attempt to approach them would no doubt be rebuffed.

The doorway darkened momentarily as the tall broad figure of Brother Bartholl Williamson, a local Society of God's Children minister and physician, entered the hospital carrying a satchel.

"Here are the old syringes you wanted to look at." His warm tenor, at odd contrast with his size, reverberated in the examining room. "I had to twist old Theo's arm to convince him to part with them for even a day."

"I probably won't keep them that long," said Abram. "I just want to see how they are designed. It's impossible to find any of these back home. The ancients insisted on making them all out of plastic for easy disposal and of course any not thrown out deteriorated away over the centuries. If we had any metal or glass ones, they were salvaged for scrap."

"A great loss," replied Bartholl, rubbing absently at an old scar on his chin. "I think it's fortunate we have these. Thank the Heavenly Creator for hoarders!"

"We have old drawings of course, but seeing the actual ones and handling them is far better. It's too bad these don't have the needles with them." Abram carefully experimented for a bit with the plunger. It still moved with relative smoothness, given that it was probably over a thousand years old. Bartholl was right. Whoever the devoted collectors were who preserved these through the generations, they had likely won themselves a good place in the afterlife.

"These would have had detachable metal needles, I think. Long since lost," the Reverend said with a tone of regret, his darkly tanned, seamed face becoming pensive. "If it were possible to regain the ability to make vaccines, we would certainly need to learn how to make these again. I know you have great hopes about that. But I just can't foresee our ever recovering the technical knowledge. So much has been lost."

His face wistful, Abram looked through all of them and finally handed them back to Bartholl, who carefully set them back into the satchel.

"Yes, but a fellow can't help dreaming. My Order has done much to preserve the old knowledge and continues working to adapt it to new conditions. As for these, well, basically they're very small pumps, so producing the syringe would be easy enough. The real problem would be making a small hollow needle." Said Abram thoughtfully. "Something that can be sterilized after each use. I find it hard to believe we can't find a use for these. Perhaps a metalsmith skilled in making small objects—"

"Doctor Abram! Reverend Bartholl!" Consuela's voice startled them both. She was standing at the doorway looking out. "There's a Christos woman coming this way!"

Both men jumped up and headed towards the door. Sure enough, a Christos, an elderly woman, her white hair trying to escape from the bright blue scarf she wore, approached, the wind playing with her faded blue tabard. Her dark brown skirt flapped around her legs. Sturdy leather boots showed much wear and dust. Originally Abram always imagined the Christos clad in dour clothing matching their equally dour culture but the reality made him discard that notion. The people he had seen in the refugee camp all wore bright skirts, kerchiefs, hats and trousers, along with red, white or blue tabards decorated with crosses and sometimes white stars on a blue or green background.

The old woman carried a blanket bundle, her thin face filled with a grim determination that drew her mouth into a narrow line and her brows into a fierce scowl. She began screeching at them in Road Talk, the common language used up and down the coast, before she even set foot on the flagstones leading to the door.

"You! You will help! You must help! They can call me apostate all they want but I will not stand by and watch my little grandson die!"

With a start, Abram realized the bundle she carried contained a small child and hurried out to meet her. And a very sick little boy he was. Perhaps two or three years old, light-skinned with ash blond hair, his listless face had sunken eyes and a ghastly pallor. The child's grandmother thrust out the bundle.

"I pour water into him but it just goes through him! It is like trying to fill a broken jug!" The old woman's voice was raspy and had the same abrasive qualities as fingernails on a chalkboard. Abram drew back the blanket and gently pinched the skin on the boy's arm. It took a long time to regain its shape. Bartholl came looking over his shoulder.

"Dehydration." The reverend pronounced.

"Is he vomiting?" Asked Abram.

"No, no," grated the old woman. "Just a flux. But it keeps coming and he keeps getting worse! They won't help back there. Claudius is the only physician among us but he has nothing with him that can help. He says it's all the will of Yehovah and tells me I should be preparing a burial shroud! No, I say! I will not accept this! I cannot believe that Yehovah wants a little boy to die!" Her voice trembled.

"Nor should you," declared Abram firmly. "Bring him inside."

They quickly brought the child in and placed him on an examination table after Consuela laid out some blankets on it.

"His electrolytes are certainly out of balance," said Abram, his expression worried, as he bent over the boy who briefly opened his eyes and stared at the Essene dully. "We should have the rehydration ingredients on hand."

"We do," said Bartholl. "I'll start preparing it at once."

"What's this?" snapped the old woman. "What are you saying?"

"My apologies," replied Abram, switching back to Road Talk. "Your grandson needs more than just water. When a child as small as he has diarrhea very badly, it causes vital substances to be lost from the body which must be replaced. The medicine's very simple to make. I'm surprised your physician doesn't know this."

"Bah! All he does is read old cures from books! I could do as much myself and probably would have. But the Redeemer clan burned us out and we had to flee with only the clothes on our backs!"

So she was a member of one of the ruling clans in the Christos territory, thought Abram. Small wonder her demeanor was so imperious. To avoid reawakening any old suspicions she might be harboring, he continued speaking in Road Talk, carefully explaining everything they were doing. She paced nervously back and forth, her anxious gaze constantly returning to her grandson. A little shrine dedicated to Saint Ravael and decorated with flowers and a small bowl of clean water sat next to the entrance. Abram had hung his little Tree of Life necklace on a corner of the shrine, where it glinted in the shaft of sunlight coming through the door. She glared at the necklace and shrine for a moment, then shook her head as if annoyed with herself. Her expression softened a bit when she saw the purring ginger cat settled on the table Abram and Bartholl had been sitting at. She glanced a moment into the satchel, frowned at the contents, then seemed to dismiss them from her mind and returned to the examination table. She finally relaxed enough to tell them the boy's name was Emmanuel and she was Gertrid, of the Salvation clan.

"We're not very important," she remarked as Bartholl brought the rehydration medicine over. "Just a small homestead, with a few farmers and crafters serving us. In fact, we're just over the border from this land. I thought we'd be safe from all the killing going on to the north of us. But they've all gone mad! Both my sons were killed in that stupid battle with the New York Commonwealth. My daughter Charity, Emmanuel's mother, died in childbirth. He's all I have left of my bloodline! You must help him!"

"We can," reassured Abram. "He just needs to keep drinking the medicine we have. Once he's improved, we can concentrate on doing something for that diarrhea." When he told her the ingredients in the rehydration formula, Gertrid squawked in aggravation.

"But that's so simple!" she sputtered. "Why couldn't that idiot Claudius know that? He sets bones and patches wounds well enough."

Abram wasn't prepared to comment on Claudius's abilities as a physician, though he suspected they were barely adequate, especially given that he seemed unaware of something as elementary as rehydration medicine.

"How many other children are sick?" he asked. "I noticed none playing today and worried."

Gertrid looked at him in surprise and then cackled.

"My grandson is the only one ill so far. No, you didn't see any running about because very early this morning a religious procession went down the road. It was one for Saint Appleseed. I've seen his idol often enough being paraded about blessing the fields just over the border where I live! But nearly everyone got into a panic over it, thinking some kind of sorcery was going on. So they hid the children away so they wouldn't get kidnapped for a sacrifice!" She cackled again when she saw Abram roll his eyes. "Oh, you wouldn't believe the rot the Congressional elders tell us all the time! I used to believe it myself when I was young and naive, but now that I'm old and wicked, I can see it's all rubbish!"

Abram laughed, finding himself warming up to this irritable old grandmother. She was certainly changing his perception of Christos. As the day passed, they kept giving Emmanuel sips of the rehydration drink and though he made a face at each mouthful, he dutifully drank it. Bit by bit the sunken look disappeared from around his eyes and he became a little more animated. The boy began insisting on taking the drink only from Gertrid, obviously uncertain what to make of the strangers gathered around him. This freed up Abram and Consuela to attend the occasional visitor, one a man who broke his arm in a fall, another a pregnant woman coming to have the midwife give her a checkup, and finally a mother and father bringing in their club-footed infant, his tiny feet held by a foot brace.

Gertrid watched the activity closely while ministering to her grandson. Her eyebrows went up as Abram gently manipulated the baby's club feet as part of an effort to gradually straighten them, then reapplied the cast on each leg to hold the foot corrections.

"I'm going to have Claudius come here!" she declared when Abram had finished. "He could learn a thing or two, I wager!"

"No doubt," said Abram dryly. "As long as you explain to him we don't eat children."

Gertrid cackled, then looked tenderly down at her grandson, who seemed much better and was now napping after hungrily consuming a cup of chicken broth. It was encouraging that Emmanuel had shown no signs of diarrhea during his stay and more importantly had begun urinating. Since a bit of color was coming back into his face, it looked as if he might recover on his own, now that he was properly rehydrated. Nourishing food and clean water would ensure that. Bartholl must have had the same thought for he came over and sat beside Abram.

"Gertrid," the reverend said, "I understand your people are frightened and suspicious of us but living in tents with no mosquito netting and no clean drinking water is a recipe for more illnesses like your grandson's. And we're only at the beginning of the hot season."

"I know that." Gertrid's expression was vexed. "Those of us who live near the border are used to your ways but some of the others are from further north and too afraid to accept any help. Though I noticed when some of the men stole netting from this place, everyone took that easily enough! Bah! As if theft was acceptable in Yehovah's eyes! They can excuse it all they like saying they are just taking from devil worshipers but the only devils I've seen are the ones who burned the home my family lived in for generations, trying to kidnap people who have loyally served me and my late husband for many years!"

She suddenly looked very old and tired.

"It's not like when I was young. Yes, we can be a hard people, but we've always tried living by the laws and holy edicts passed on to us by our ancestors. But something's gotten twisted. My heart tells me this is not how it should be but what can be done to change it? Many welcomed Daniel of the Savior clan when he and his people fought and overthrew the Prophet clan. The Prophets were the ones who passed a dreadful edict years ago saying deformed children must be exposed or crucified. Yehovah, what a horrible thing! Yet almost no one dared defy them. Only the Savior clan did! They claimed they found old written records showing that poison glowing metal caused the deformities and not Yehovah's wrath at all. They were able to get everyone to rally behind them saying the Prophets had deliberately suppressed that knowledge so they could maintain control by keeping people afraid all the time. Oh, what a battle that was!

"But after the Savior clan took over and rescinded the edict, all Daniel could talk about was becoming a great power! Why ever should we care for such a thing? I think he got that into his head after seeing the great masted ships of the Commonwealths sailing in the distance. And then that flying machine they had! There was nothing for it but we had to build one too! Daniel wanted to borrow my metalsmith and his sons to make the parts for it because they're the best anywhere, but I wouldn't have anything to do with it. I'm no fool. I'd never get those people back! And all for what? Just to show the Commonwealths anything they can do, we can do better? What rot! Well, he finally managed to get one built but he did it by sending soldiers into the south here, grabbing all the scrap metal they could, instead of trading for it like honest people. Then he stole the engine for it from the New York Commonwealth. Well, Yehovah knows how to reward people like that. It crashed somewhere in the Palachian mountains, and good riddance, I say!"

Abram gulped a bit as she spoke, remembering when he had been among the Palachian people two years before. The little Christos plane had been flying over the mountain villages attacking, swooping low, trying to terrorize them. A lucky aim from his slingshot had caused the pilot to lose control and crash, killing him, something that still weighed heavily on Abram's conscience. He kept silent though, letting Gertrid continue talking. It was clear she had not been able to confide her feelings to anyone for a long time.

"Now Jeremiah, of the Penance clan, has shown up. I've never liked him; his family's always bragging about how they are the most pious and should be the ones leading the Congressional Elders. Ha! It's like my own granny used to say; those who talk about it the most do it the least! Apparently Yehovah doesn't think they're worthy either, since the word came to us just before we got attacked, that his clan got soundly trounced by the Apostolic clan after they tried snatching some territory from them. Ever since Daniel got killed, it seems like everyone is paying back old grudges or trying to gain some advantage at someone else's expense. No one's cooperating any more. I don't understand how it can all go to pieces so quickly!"

She reached into her pocket and pulled out a gleaming gold coin.

"Jeremiah has been flashing these at the two guards I have left, trying to lure them and some of my other people into some hare-brained scheme he has. He dropped this and didn't notice, so I grabbed it. I suppose that makes me a thief now as well." She tossed it morosely onto the table.

Something about the sound of the coin striking the wood and the coin's appearance caught Abram's attention. He had seen and even handled gold coins back in his homeland. Somehow this coin didn't look right. He picked it up and noted its light weight. But it was the design of the coin that raised his eyebrows. Gertrid's sharp eyes spotted his expression.

"What is it? You look like you just ate something sour!"

"This coin looks exactly like the aluminum coins used here in Richmound," remarked Abram, his suspicions beginning to grow. He picked up a small knife and scraped at the coin. The gold quickly yielded to a silvery gleam.

"Well, now, it's definitely our local cent!" said Bartholl, taking the coin and looking it over. "It has gold leaf overlaid on it but that's all."

Gertrid sprang to her feet, livid with fury. She began stamping back and forth, cursing in Road Talk at first, then Christos when she ran out of expletives. The Christos version of Old English had enough in common with other versions that Abram recognized a few of the colorful oaths she spewed. Both he and Bartholl let her vent. The tirade ended when Emmanuel woke and, frightened by his grandmother's anger, began crying. That brought her up short and she rushed over to comfort him. Once he had quieted and finally dozed off, she returned to where Abram and Bartholl sat. The anger had left her face, replaced with the steely determination they had seen when she first arrived that morning.

"I'm not going to let that walking serpent steal away what's left of my grandson's patrimony. If it was only me, I wouldn't bother trying to start over, especially at my age, but I've got to do something for his sake!"

"It may be futile confronting this rascal," warned Bartholl. "He's likely to have a few real gold coins that would put the lie to any accusation you make against him."

"Oh, I'm not going to accuse him," smiled Gertrid grimly. "I have my own ideas on how to face him. But I want the two of you to come with me."

Bartholl and Abram exchanged puzzled glances, but then Bartholl stood up.

"Madam, I am a minister of the Society of God's Children and Doctor Abram is an Essene, a holy order dedicated to healing and the harmonizing of the body and soul with our Mother Earth. As long as you don't ask us to do violence to anyone, we'll support you."

Gertrid cackled.

"Don't worry about that. All the two of you have to do is stand there. I'll do the rest."

Before they left, Gertrid gave a long list of instructions to Consuela on how to look after Emmanuel. The midwife took it all with surprising aplomb considering she had children of her own and knew perfectly well how to babysit. Abram smiled inwardly at Gertrid's deeply ingrained habit of giving orders. He could only hope it would help accomplish whatever it was she had in mind.

He and Bartholl followed Gertrid as she strode towards the Christos encampment. Abram could see a flurry of activity among the Christos when it became apparent they were approaching. The first person to confront them was a lean grizzled old man wearing the padded clothing of a soldier and carrying a spear. He attempted to look formidable but his padding was badly tattered and the spear had been broken and repaired. He also sported a dreadful black eye Abram yearned to put a compress on. The old man blocked their way and began speaking sternly in Christos but Gertrid interrupted him.

"Use Road Talk, you old poop!" she snapped. "These aren't devil worshipers, they're physicians and worship Yehovah just as well as we do. They saved my grandson's life and I'm bringing them here to look at our sick and injured. Claudius can't do it all himself!"

The old man's face went through some interesting contortions but his life-long habit of deference to one of Gertrid's station won out.

"I see the sense of what you're saying, Lady Gertrid," said the old soldier finally. "But Jeremiah—"

"That skunk! Who did you serve for thirty years, Zekiel, him or me? You got that black eye fighting off some of the Redeemers who wanted to snatch my craft workers for themselves! So why are you now doing what Jeremiah says? Do you really think I'm apostate just because I wanted to find someone who could heal my grandson?"

"No, of course not," replied Zekiel, his weathered face flushing. "But Jeremiah's got that soldier of his, Timaus, backing him up. Timaus's got a broken wrist and other injuries but he's half my age. Nathaniel's still laid up with that knife wound. After all we've been through, I'm not sure I could take Timaus on by myself."

"Timaus's only serving Jeremiah because of those gold coins! But I wager I can get him to come around once I give Jeremiah a piece of my mind. Now let me by!" Without waiting for Zekiel to move, she pushed past him, continuing towards the refugee camp. Zekiel made no effort to stop her but stepped aside and waited until Bartholl and Abram walked past before he began following them, a nonplussed expression on his face.

By now, the camp was definitely in an uproar, many people staring in open hostility, others looking uncertain and, curiously, some even hopeful. A rotund man, his florid face surrounded by a curly black beard, wearing a deep blue tabard decorated with crosses over a brown tunic and breeches tied with a woven belt, emerged from the crowd.

"Jeremiah, you fraud!" shouted Gertrid. "I thought they would have thrown you out of the camp by now! I didn't find any devil worshipers just some good doctors who already have helped Emmanuel. So don't you go calling me apostate now! Everybody knows devils only hurt, not help. If we weren't all so damned proud, we would have gotten help already instead of living like miserable dogs in this place!"

"Now Lady Gertrid, I know you're upset but someone has to make sure our people here don't stray from the One True Path—"

"Well, now! So you're a Law-Giver, are you?" sniffed Gertrid. "Where are the elders who appointed you, I'd like to know? Did you pass the exams? I hope they didn't notice you wrote the answers on your arms under the sleeves!"

Enough of the Christos knew Road Talk so that Abram heard a few snickers from the crowd. Jeremiah obviously didn't command the respect Gertrid did. But then perhaps it wasn't necessary. A huge hulking man, with close cropped blond hair and cold blue eyes, came up behind him. Judging from the sling on his left arm, this had to be Timaus. It was easy to see why Zekiel wasn't anxious to confront him. Jeremiah's cheeks reddened at Gertrid's taunt but he remained composed and even smiled a bit, looking down his nose at her.

As Gertrid continued upbraiding him, his smile became a smirk. Jeremiah clearly felt he had the high ground. Abram could feel a cold anger forming at the pit of his stomach and he strove to master it. It wouldn't do to lose his temper, especially given how tense the situation already was. He became aware of the gentle touch of Bartholl's hand on his elbow. The older, more experienced preacher radiated a calm confidence that helped Abram relax more. Still, the supercilious expression on Jeremiah's face was hard to take. His brief acquaintance with Gertrid had left him with a deep respect for her and the sight of this scoundrel all but spitting in her face was enough to make anyone's blood boil. He wondered what Gertrid was trying to accomplish with all her scolding.

It turned out both he and Jeremiah underestimated the matriarch of the Salvation clan. Gertrid had been inching closer to the other Christos, shaking her finger as she spoke when suddenly she lunged forward, seizing a pouch dangling from Jeremiah's belt. She tore it away with such force his belt snapped, his trousers dropping indecorously, though his tabard saved him from being completely exposed. Titters of laughter began rising in volume while the red-faced Jeremiah struggled to pull his breeches back up. Interestingly, Timaus made no effort to intervene, the faint ghost of a smile tugging at his rough face.

Gertrid took what turned out to be Jeremiah's money pouch and flung it as hard as she could at the ground. Abram was quick to notice she chose a heavily graveled area. Bright gold coins burst from the pouch and she at once began stamping furiously on them. It didn't take much abrasion from the gravel to expose the underlying base metal of the coins. He started grinning at Gertrid's simple but effective strategy. She had counted on Jeremiah being distracted by the presence of the two physicians so he wouldn't notice her moving towards his money pouch.

Gertrid scooped up the false gold coins and showed them around, shrilling at everyone in Christos. She shoved the coins into Timaus's face, her tone becoming mocking. The soldier's expression changed from shock to fury. Abram looked towards Jeremiah to see how he was taking this. However, like many con men before him, the Christos realized the jig was up and was already fleeing. Timaus turned and began pursuing, a short sword suddenly in his hand, but his injuries had him limping too badly and he soon gave up the chase. Many of the other Christos made up for it, though, by continuing the pursuit and pelting Jeremiah with stones. Yelping with pain, the miscreant picked up speed and soon disappeared from sight.

The Christos lost no time going through Jeremiah's tent to see what he had left behind. As Bartholl had predicted, only a few coins were genuine gold; the rest were Richmound cents with gold leaf, some of it already flaking off. Timaus confiscated the real gold but then presented it to Gertrid, speaking to her in an apologetic tone. Many of the Christos who had greeted their approach with hostility now looked sad and confused, whatever hopes Jeremiah had raised dashed. Gertrid quickly took them in hand, instructing them to allow Abram and Bartholl to examine them, her raspy voice, surprisingly, taking on a quiet and reassuring tone. Many hung back at first, still suspicious, but bit by bit a few began coming forward under Lady Gertrid's stern eye.

"Some of them have been telling me that rat was promising them they could go back home safely again after he bribed a few people there with his coins," Gertrid said while the two doctors inspected the Christos she brought to them. "But I can't imagine things being safe enough for that, even if he did have the money! I daresay he had a few friends with ropes and chains waiting across the border and all these poor souls would have found themselves illegally indentured, probably for the rest of their lives!"

"And Jeremiah would make a fat profit from selling them," said Abram, shaking his head, not bothering to hide the surge of anger he felt. The ugly business of turning petty criminals doing limited indentured service into permanent slaves, and then selling them away far to the south, was an old problem here. Displaced people like the Christos would be vulnerable to this criminal practice. The woman, whose bruised arm he was examining, apparently understood Road Talk, for she turned white with shock as they spoke. She began sobbing quietly.

"What's to become of us, then?" She looked pleadingly at Bartholl and Gertrid, her eyes brimming with tears. "Where are we to go?"

"Don't you have land around here that no one uses?" asked a squirrely-looking young man, clutching what had to be the most battered satchel Abram ever saw. It looked as if it would fall apart at any moment but its owner held it closely, probably the only possession he had. "If we can't go back home again, surely there is room for us here?"

"Ah, Claudius," smiled Gertrid. "That's a good question."

"There's former pastureland up by the aqueducts," said Abram, looking at Bartholl. "It doesn't belong to anyone that I'm aware of. Perhaps they could move there, at least temporarily. It's certainly better than this place. It's higher up, with better drainage, and the aqueduct waters are clean. It's still early enough so they could plant some food for themselves." He looked at the Christos woman he had been tending. "I think you'll find people here very generous. You can get chickens, goats, whatever you need if you only ask."

"Actually, the area is part of the commons of the city," replied Bartholl. "But they retired it to allow it to regenerate for a few years. I don't think they will mind it being used for one season. In the meantime, I can talk to the city elders. There's land under the ownership of Richmound to the north of us that's empty but fertile. It hasn't been designated as a commons and it's recently been pronounced clear of pollution so it would make a good place to live. It's near the border but you should be safe enough, though you may have to put up with the occasional nuisance of a Saint Appleseed blessing. They're very popular around here."

"Oh, foo!" sniffed Gertrid. "If that's the worse thing that happens, I suspect I'll be doing well. I just want to make a life for my grandson. Our own land is stolen and I don't think we'll ever get it back." She dabbed at her eyes, trying to fight back sudden tears. It gave Abram a pang to see the sorrow on that proud old face. "I can see there are kind people here. If I don't live long enough, well, at least I'll know he's in good hands. I've still got my metal workers, some farmers, and a few guards. We'll make it."

Three days later, Abram sat behind the little hospital meditating, taking advantage of a quiet spell. Rain showers had passed by, leaving a fresh moist aroma behind along with gleaming puddles. The rich scents of the herb garden from which he drew his more common medicines tickled his nostrils. The ginger cat, now dubbed Tripper by Consuela, crouched beside a large flower pot, focusing on a spot where a vole had disappeared. Abram suspected the cat would be disappointed as the vole likely used a tunnel under the pot and had long since made its getaway. The sound of Consuela bustling about, humming to herself as she swept up the floor of the sick bed area, made a pleasing counterpoint to the birds calling.

The sound of Brother Bartholl's feet on the floorboards announced his presence.

"Ah, I hope I'm not interrupting," said the minister, stepping out into the garden.

"Not at all," replied Abram. "Just meditating. Gertrid came by earlier to collect Emmanuel. I thought for a while Tripper might have to go with him. He became very attached to our little mouser."

"From what Consuela told me, he was quite a fireball once he recovered," chuckled Bartholl.

"Considering who his grandmother is, that isn't surprising. She's going to have her hands full." Abram smiled briefly. Brother Bartholl noted the pensive expression on his face.

"Is something troubling you?"

"Well, no, not exactly. I'm just wrestling with some old problems. My tendency to judge people and my hot temper."

"Have no fear, Brother Abram," smiled Bartholl. "You're still young and will outgrow both as our Creator guides you through your life." He tapped the small scar on his chin. "Someday I'll tell you how I got this. It's from a time in my life I'm not too proud of, but it started me on a better path. You managed your temper very well the other day. And as for judging others, well, let's face it, the Christos don't really make it easy for us, do they?"

"I feel grateful meeting Lady Gertrid, at any rate," said Abram. "She gave a human face to the Christos I needed to see."

"The council has alloted a parcel of land for Lady Gertrid and her people so they can build a small homestead . I'm sorry to say many of the Christos have gone to other refugee camps but enough have stayed with her so she will be able to set up housekeeping fairly quickly."

"Yes, she told me about getting some land. I'm glad to hear it," said Abram. "I'm not surprised many of the refugees didn't take up the offer, especially after a lifetime being told we're nothing but devil worshipers. Change can be painful even if you are ready for it."

Someone noisily hemming and hawing made them look up. The Christos physician Claudius stood in the doorway looking timid as a schoolboy, still clutching his satchel.

"Lady Consuela told me you were out here," he quavered. "Lady Gertrid suggested I come and see you."

"I have a feeling it was more than a suggestion," laughed Abram, gesturing at him to come sit. "I think our methods here impressed her quite a bit."

"Yes," replied Claudius, brightening. "She told me how you were helping a club-footed child. I would very much like to see that." As he walked, Abram noticed he had a slight limp. He looked about his own age. His thin frame showed signs of poor nutrition early in life, though his face was animated enough. "I had a mentor when I was younger but he died of tuberculosis before he fully trained me. I tried educating myself with Lady Gertrid's library but that's all burned now."

"It's better to learn from experience," said Abram. "But there are many libraries here with old books, many in Old English. I can probably find a few for you."

"Oh that would be wonderful!" said Claudius. He looked down at his battered satchel. "The attack happened so suddenly I could only grab this. I wish I had gotten some of the books instead. Many were quite old."

He opened the satchel and pulled out a hypodermic syringe. Abram realized it wasn't an ancient relic but a new one, tipped with a long thin needle. He stared at it, fascinated.

"May I look at that?"

"Of course. I had Simon the metalworker make it for me. He copied it from a book illustration I showed him. But it's too big to really be any good."

Abram realized that as he examined it. Still, the craftsmanship was superb. The plunger moved effortlessly. The needle and syringe body were all one piece, with the needle having a small hole at the end of it. He began understanding better why Lady Gertrid's homestead had been targeted by attackers and why their now-dead leader had approached her for metalworking. *I should have realized she wasn't just bragging,* he chuckled to himself. *Not very important, indeed.* Her metalworkers must have been the envy of everyone in the Christos territory.

"It does work quite well for squirting medicine in the mouths of reluctant animals and children, but I wouldn't dare try using it to inject anything the way the books showed. But Simon did such a good job on my leg brace, I thought perhaps he could make something like the syringe."

"A leg brace?" said Bartholl. "If it's not impolite to ask, may we see?"

"Oh, I don't mind at all," said Claudius. He wore a long brown robe with a little caduceus embroidered near the shoulder—the Christos version of a doctor's robes, Abram supposed. Claudius lifted it up, revealing an elaborate leather and metal leg brace encasing his left leg.

"I had an illness several years ago that caused me to lose the use of much of my leg. But Simon made the brace so I could walk. It actually stood up quite well to the long journey we took here when we escaped. It's started to become hard to move a bit, though. I don't know how I'll get it repaired if it breaks. Simon and his family lost all their tools in the attack."

"Claudius, you can tell Simon he and his sons can get all the tools they need here. This is marvelous work," said Abram, admiring the carefully crafted hinges, padded with cotton to prevent chafing.

"I agree," added Bartholl. "It's better than any of the ones I've seen here or up north in the Commonwealths."

"Really?" Claudius blinked in surprise.

"Yes," said Abram, smiling. "In fact, I can think of several people here who could use such a leg brace. Tell Lady Gertrid if she can get her metalworkers producing again, her grandson's patrimony is assured."

"Bless me! She'll be happy to hear that."

"Doctors," said Consuela, emerging out of the hospital door carrying a bowl of sliced strawberries. "My sister sent over some fresh berries. I thought you might want a little something to eat first. A runner just came saying they're bringing in a man who broke both his legs. I wasn't told how it happened but I'm sure we'll find out."

"Oh my!" everyone said at once, for Consuela had used Road Talk for their visitor's benefit. Claudius blushed, but Abram laughed.

"Well, now's as good a time as any to start," he said. "I'm sure you already know how to set bones but you'll need to be able to tell Lady Gertrid we kept you busy. Thank you, Consuela."

"That's Lady Consuela to you," she replied archly as she went back inside.

"I wasn't sure what the correct term of address was for her," said Claudius, blushing again. "I didn't want to cause offense."

"I think you pleased her immensely," said Bartholl, smiling. "We're quite informal here. But come, my friends. Enough talk. Let's enjoy these berries first before we get too busy to eat anything else."

Ghosts of Greenland

by Alistair Herbert

THE OLDER I GOT, THE MORE OBVIOUS IT FELT that the place was trying to say something—to tell *me* something. It was like the way a song or a shout resonates in your head after it ends; like imagining you just heard something very loud. It was a voice I heard at distance, no way to pick out words, maybe no words in the first place, but speaking anyway. It was familiar and strange at the same time. The place changed me into a fox, changed me into a bird, changed me into compost, and it spoke to me constantly until I began to listen.

I couldn't discuss it with anyone, but I still felt it. I hardly talked to Mum at all; Mum wanted me in a hospital which didn't exist here, and she hated us both for it. Dad took me walking, exploring near home; he said it was the only hobby he brought with him from his own home, and the longer my legs grew the further we could go. We didn't much talk; he took my side at the expense of his marriage, and made sure he didn't find reason to doubt that I would be okay. We mapped out the landscape together and I felt myself slowly approaching the voice, tracking it out through the valley.

The hills south of the house—south of the river—called me for longest. From the house, low by the river, you hardly saw them: they seemed lower than our own bank's slopes. We had to cross the bridge and choose a path up from the road near the new farmhouse before we could see beyond the false summit, the flat fields and the real stuff rising beyond it. The journey to the top and back took half a day; we would diverge in one direction or another and pick our way over at height, then find a way back where it suited us. The village proper was further south, and anyone there with leisure time would head east for the reservoir; we rarely met anyone.

To me this place was always home, but to them it was only ever a foreign country, a thing they clumsily tried to learn. Dad got here early; bought the land while it was still half-frozen, held onto it, eventually put in his saplings and waited for them to make soil from the thin air, and later miraculous fruit—all at the same time, the year before I was born—and then he moved. While his colleagues spent their money on holidays, curries, and gold, he was modestly frugal, investing everything he had in Greenland, waiting for it to justify its name. But he was forty years old by the time he actually moved, and you don't just uproot yourself like that without losing something.

We lumbered around in all weather. If it rained he would come home sodden, but he didn't seem to mind. His coat was at once futuristic and archaic: old shiny black material which crinkled under the hand and billowed like a bag in heavy wind. The trousers matched, and from behind he was a melting black candle—hard to see anything human there if I didn't already know it was him. He would emerge hot and wet from sweat; after rain deep patches of darkened fabric covered his shoulders and chest. *It's all part of the adventure*, he said. *If you're not miserable at some point then you're not on an adventure.* We called him daft. He couldn't leave the place he left behind; he had to continually confront himself with his culture's lunacy, inviting hardship. Holly, always more sure of her place than either me or our father, mocked him, and apologised for him with a snigger when her friends visited. I dreamed about the place he left behind, as if it was another of his ancient stories, part of a saga, and not a place which was still there, still full of people busily controlling the world.

A cloudburst hit us as we passed the bridge. We tried to shelter by the old wall —*This is ridiculous*, he said—and it kept going for several minutes as we stood in the grass and endured the attack. When it stopped he shouted in triumph, as if we'd somehow beaten the rain by surviving it, and we climbed the hill into air which was hard to describe: the kind of air you only get when the rain's so heavy it's knocked everything out of the sky. It left behind half-black clouds and breaks of clear blue sky, spots of water still dropping in pairs as if it only occurred to them to fall after the storm had finished.

We climbed the second slope; trickles crossed the path, running down the dirt for a few yards and looking for somewhere to turn back onto the steeper slope. Here you could almost imagine people didn't exist, with the new farmhouse sneaking under the lower slope's arm. Where the path flattens we met a doubled rainbow sliding down from the fog at the edge of the cloud bank and halving the sky as it landed in the valley, one of its four legs planted barely a hundred yards above us in the rocks. It was unbelievably bright; a pointed finger from a god I doubt exists.

We chased it with unspoken agreement; it was fading even as we started. We dropped to cross a crease and found reed-edged water moving across our way; I sank in, and knew before I pulled back that I would be muddy halfway up my shin, but the boot came up clean. Dad plunged on ahead of me. We aimed for a crop of loose rocks on the hill edge, and it looked like the rainbow's inner band was tangled somewhere in its south-west corner, nestled just behind this one and in front of that one. The rainbow moved and settled. I moved ahead, stomping hard along my own line to make up the distance I'd lost in the reeds. I looked to check he was still there and saw him hopping along, a rain-slicked jackdaw in a plastic coat. A cloud ate the rainbow and it wisped away to leave nothing but clear air, green grass, blue water. In the world before I was born this place was frozen. He laughed, soaked already in the usual places, feeling his age now that I could match his stride. The hill was steeper than it looked from the other side; I knew that he half wanted to call it a day and I didn't; he had work waiting when we went home; I dragged him on by refusing to look back.

And there in the rocks was   just sitting in shelter.

What, she said as I stopped dead in front of her. I watched her face and its hundred messages. The rainbow's end was gone, and obviously she hadn't seen it anyway from her direction. Her face asked why I was looking at her so amazed. A girl just sitting; her being in a place like that became awkward with someone seeing her. I was feeling my understanding of the world change, but I had no idea what to say. He saved us, tripping and booming a greeting as he caught me and saw her. He said something dull about the downpour, to which she nodded, still watching me warily. We might have been the same age; I was her peer, and my Dad was just another creature. We stood for a bare moment and he caught his breath and recalled himself; neutral smile on panting face, mouth open, eyes squinting slightly. *Come on then, Will*, he said, *let's see if we can't get back down before it begins again.*

Even if I thought of it, I wouldn't have known how to ask her who she was. I left her and when Dad tried to talk on the way down the slope I started to trot, dropped to four legs, smelled out the right paths home, and he couldn't do anything but watch me disappear in the tall grass, and find me back at home, sulking near the locked larder.

I spent the winter moping in my room, and doing Dad's chores while he worked away—his old colleagues had found him some work he could do from the coastal library. When the clouds made bad weather for hawks and hunters I risked the occasional outing, but I knew it was wrong to change shape; it wasn't what I ought to be doing, so I tried not to do it. It wasn't for Mum. I didn't even want to turn into an animal. Every story I knew warned me away from it.

It was spring before I saw her again, and that first meeting barely counts for anything. I went looking when the evenings brightened, and back up there among the rocks I found all sorts—foil packets, strange flowers, gutted fires, four legged creatures, black and white feathers, remnants of pornographic magazines, bad weather, false clues, rabbit droppings—maybe twenty-five years since the melt, and litter and birds and young trees had already claimed the place. I didn't see her.

When I did see her, though, I was ready; we were in the village, I was carrying the groceries for Mum, and   shrugged past us plucking small items from the shelves. She left without paying, as if she hadn't taken anything, and didn't see me, or didn't know me. *I'll be back for the bus*, I said, deciding instantly, and deliberately not hearing Mum's answering question; I knew I was leaving her with too much to carry, but I had to follow. I had been thinking about it. I moved quickly along the street, the sun pleasant on my skin but not warming the chill from the air. I turned crow-like; I hopped wide and ragged into the hedgerow and flapped and fluttered between branches, trying to keep her in sight. I needed the disguise, but it was almost impossible to follow her as a bird. With most targets, as a crow, you narrow the possible courses and you track those where the air lets you. But humans will do anything at any time; they don't make proper sense. She would walk the pavement, I guessed, but as soon as she left the high street there was no telling where she might flit or wander.

She set out across a field; I slipped down from my last tree and stepped out to follow her, knowing by now she would see I wasn't hunting her as a shoplifter, briefly enjoying the feeling of walking behind her without her knowing—but of course she knew, and she turned to confront me. I had forgotten what her face looked like.

You're following me, she said. *Yes*, I said. *Why. Because I can*, I said. I felt surer than I was. I had decided being sure I deserved a thing was the best way to get it—far better than trying to earn it with honesty. Her face was so serious. We might have been the same age, but she just as easily could have been one of the rocks the place was made from. Or maybe all teenagers are so serious—and only conceal it for fear of mockery, and only don't recognise it in themselves.

Why *was* I following her? The rainbow pointed her out and I stopped dead when I saw her, as though every corner of my mind was swept clean in a moment on the rocks. I was thirteen and alive and the world was one long question never to be answered, and she just turned up into it. She was thin and fierce. I felt she was part of me even if the reverse happened not to be true.

Come and see me, I said. *Along near the river. I have to go help my mum with the bus, but come and see me.* She said, *You live near the old house.* I nodded, and she asked, *What's your name. Will. You?*   *. So why would I come and see you. You're private*, I said, *you like to hide on the hills and stay out of your folks' hair. I don't care about mine.* She shook her head and rolled her eyes. *Not why would I come to you instead of you to me. Why would I see you at all. We're not friends.* I looked at her. The field was grass waiting for summer to grow it, the sky grey overhead. The metal fence marked a boundary. I tried to guess which house was hers—where she was going. *Do you remember the rainbow the first day I saw you? What rainbow. There was a rainbow*, I said. *It pointed me to you.* She didn't respond. *So let's be friends.* I could tell she was thinking, but not about what. *How did you follow me* *without me knowing until just now*, she asked. *I ran. No you didn't. Okay. I turned into a crow and flew after you.* She smirked the way we smirk when suspecting a joke. We stood for a few moments in silence. *Do you know the lost house*, she asked at last, *the lost mall.* I nodded. *It's halfway. You might see me there some time.*

I let her go. It felt like sunbathing. It felt like stillness after sex, with the whole world in quiet balance. It felt like I had just won a fight with an unbeatable opponent. I ran to catch my mother at the bus, and barely made it.

The lost mall is outside the village in a nothing place: the three roads form a junction surrounding a triangle wasteland and two buildings. The north-west road passes our house on the river, the one east and south forks to the village and eventually town, and the south road reaches down to other villages and sees no traffic. Inside the triangle stands what we call the lost mall.

Dad says for a time people thought Greenland could be the new Rome, and the electric toys and offices could migrate here along with the people. They built these huge malls in every town, and it seemed like the more malls they built, the more money they had. Even a village like ours could have a mall. They flattened saplings people had just planted, re-sited young roads, and brought in these concrete palaces, but they usually failed; it made no sense to build things out of town, when people preferred not to travel. Our mall never even opened, but the building still stands, in a wide open space for cars which never existed. Trees are muscling up through it, or maybe down through it, slowly.

There's a house, too, just inside the southern corner; I don't know why, but that's where I saw ⬜⬜⬜⬜, just as she said. She gave me a tour, showed me the ways in, and I felt, from there, with her to talk to, I was a spider web's distance from making sense of it all. I'm not sure what I mean by *it all*.

We went to the house, or what used to be its gardens, and we went to the mall. We climbed the fire ladder to a badly boarded window on the north face, from which you could get inside and wander the corridors in the half-light between the closed metal shutters. From the inner courtyard you could reach a service staircase to the roof. It was designed for electric light, so when the door closed behind you it was dark; you climbed two flights with your hands out before dim grey light hung through a glass door into the main mall space. Eventually you bumped into the roof door.

She kissed me while we stood looking down towards the river and the trees which hid my house. I think she had been waiting for me to kiss her. The hills stretched beyond, the other side of the valley in the opposite direction, and as far as the outcrop where we met. The smoke haze marked the village. Somewhere to the east I knew there was an ocean. You could look at the river and then look at the grey haze, and think how this water would become that water. I wondered if it had once been ice. I don't think we were girlfriend and boyfriend, though sometimes that whole thing lurked in one or the other of our voices. We cared less than older people would care; the way each other's skin felt was a sideshow to our unendingly trying to explain to each other ourselves, this place, this whole thing going on around us for who knows what reason. Who we were, where we fit, how it felt jumping into water or climbing darkened towers or being in each other's company; we were busy.

I told her about my family falling apart. My parents barely spoke; Mum had her friend there almost as often as I was there; Dad seemed to go off walking for longer at a time, with less to say when he arrived home. Holly and I distanced ourselves from the fighting, but we still took sides. Holly wanted to try and hold things together; I thought she should let them fight. What did I care, I argued, if they hated each other? *They can't hate each other*, she said, over and over again. *Something's gone wrong and all of us need to fix it*. She was eleven years old and she dominated the conversation at dinner time—sought praise, gave it, prevented any chore going undone. I think she thought that, if she could keep us in one place, she could fit us back together when things calmed down. She knew things would calm down. I went off as often as I could, leaving her there alone. Their war, I saw, predated us; I couldn't see the cause, but I felt sure something lingered unseen and unmended. And one day he didn't come home at all when we had thought that he would.

Mum was tight-lipped. *I'm not a part of this*, her face said, not meeting our eyes, so bullish that it was obvious she didn't believe it herself. After three days he was still gone. Holly went through his things and found nothing missing; there was a book he'd started, folded open beside his bed, a letter he'd left unanswered. Holly thought some accident must have happened, so we went out searching his favourite high places. But this place is too big to search; from every peak there's another peak, more young farms, more water. Later she found an empty space where his tent should have been. *See*, she said, *he went on holiday and forgot to tell us, he'll be back next week*. Mum said nothing. I laughed. *He's not forgotten anything—he likes the hills and he decided to never come back. Or else he's stowing away on a boat home*. Holly left the room, face contorted, and I told myself I didn't care.

          said it was strange I would sympathise with him. The house was quiet now Holly had stopped trying to fix it, and it seemed clear enough to   that you stand by the person who stands by you, not the one who leaves. *Whatever goes on*, she said, *you don't know everything about your parents' lives. There's too much between you and them, so the only way you can be fair is with basic rules. Like what*, I asked. *Like the one who leaves is the one you blame*. We were on the lost mall's roof looking at a pink-orange sunset under stretched and thinning clouds; the shadows were lengthening, and the short, wild summer was almost over. While I slacked off, Holly would be canning strawberries and stewing rhubarb. Couldn't I see from here how fragile everything was, how uncertain every connection, how temporary? ▮▮▮▮▮ found these questions urgent: she was angry. Didn't I want to keep growing?

I told her that wasn't the point. I knew about being pragmatic, but I wouldn't be pragmatic with my family's story, here where I only told it to her and myself. *Okay*, she said, *but you're still wrong to favour him. One parent ran and one stayed. Which one is in your house now? You don't understand*, I told her. *Okay*, she said again. *I don't understand. What don't I understand. Make me understand.*

I started to tell her, and I waited for her to leave too.

I told her how Mum ran off before, when I was tiny, and then came back; how it was all because I turned into a fox; how I still hadn't stopped myself doing it completely; how I wasn't all human; how Mum thought it was in my imagination, and why wouldn't I stop; how she hunted remedies and nothing worked, and all she wanted was to be back in Glasgow-on-Sea and near the proper hospitals which, thanks to my Dad's career suicide, she'd never see again; how it wasn't in my imagination and a hospital wouldn't help; how it was a question of simple willpower I was slowly practising. The sun went down. We began to feel the chill of next month coming, and I knew she would suffer from her parents for returning home late, but she just sat and listened.

I didn't show her; I knew indulging it would only bring me back inside it. I know how addiction works—how you think surely just once can't hurt, and then you're back in the circle. But I told her everything I remembered: everything I saw myself, every guess at my future, all the worries mum had whispered to me when she didn't think I was old enough to understand. *It's like a dream*, I said, when at last I'd finished the story. *And I know it's real. And I know it's always there waiting to consume me.*

Her mouth opened and the voice followed a few moments later. It felt like I was watching her solving a jigsaw puzzle, holding each piece for a moment above the board before being set down. A game of chess. A moment of aiming before you throw the stone. I wanted to pull her close and realised I had no idea what to do with her once our bodies were touching. My cheeks were cold.

This was the first time she had heard about this; the only time I told anyone. She didn't say it was far-fetched, which was what I expected: some healthy scepticism, or that it was crazy, or that I needed help.

How do you know, she asked, *that it's the fox that's the dream?*

I didn't.

How do you know you weren't always a fox, and then one day you started to dream that you were a person?

I don't.

You have to admit, this whole thing with the houses full of machines, the boats and the wars and the malls, the unhappy people trying to please each other by hurting them—it's all a bit unlikely, isn't it?

It is.

That's not exactly comforting, I told her. *Oh I'm sorry*, she murmured, her body closer and her voice further away than when she began the question. *Was I supposed to comfort you?*

And it struck me she was the only person I knew, the only person in the world, and being for a moment human felt suddenly lucky. I reached for her and found that, when they touched, each body knew for itself what to do with the other.

From there I thought different thoughts.

I tried changing again, shedding my fear of removing my awkward clothing, and tried to think about it from the fox's side for a change. In changing, though, I lost the thinking I thought I wanted; I didn't care what things meant while I was running. If a thought like this even occurred to me I would have ignored it. I wondered later about the time I chased   between trees; how did I carry my wanting between shapes? Was it even a human desire to begin with?

I went out walking and listening alone. I forgot words; I followed my feet and my nose. I remembered the rainbow in the rocks and the way it had pulled me, and I started to pick up on other signs: a breeze; a shape in stone; a feeling in my ears.

I went again towards the rocks. It was on a dry day and the breeze was low. I ended up quite far west, a little way south of the river. It was somewhere I'd not been before. At length I stopped in front of a tree, not knowing exactly why I had stopped, or why in this place. I wasn't learning how to follow the signs so much as remembering. It seemed obvious—equally obvious that, of all those possible signs, this tree was the one which ought to belong to me. It was a fir, plain and young, with a straight trunk. But it seemed out of place. I sat and listened.

Once the cacophony of birds and leaves and water settled into rhythm, I learned to settle my own breath as well. I saw how much noise my own body made, and became more attentive. A few hours later, I picked out a trace of the song the earth was singing: the thing the dirt and air had been trying to tell me the whole of my life.

Here, it said. *Here, here, here.*

I didn't even know yet what it meant. It was as if I lived in deafness, believing for all my life that the world made no sound.

You're waiting for me to tell you the magic trick. I found something in the tree. Some symbol, some clue. A nest of foxes. But that's not how it works. When you go looking, what you find is what you bring with you.

‡‡

I sat with the tree all day. In the sun I was a boy; I watched ants, and fought the urge to move and check that no ants were crawling on my skin. I felt the hardness of the tree against my back and I looked down the slope, the other trees and things continuing with their life. I began to feel that I wasn't a bird. I continued sitting. Afternoon came and went; I felt cold in my fingers and hunger in my stomach. Water moving nearby. The cold dirt in my roots. What would a tree do, I wondered, if it wanted to move, or to be something else?

I had thought it was the fox, if any part of me, which roamed unwanted. The crow I had taught about hawks and human pain, and I had it mostly under control; no creature can live with thinking about pain the way most humans think about pain. The fox crept out still, though I had tried not to acknowledge it.

I sat and watched the trees drink water, almost touching. ████████ had said the fox was only the more visible defector, that the boy was also carrying out his business without keeping me informed. That since the time before I knew what I was doing, without later learning what it was that I was doing, I had accepted as my truth something which was only a story—a way of making sense of something which shouldn't ever make sense.

The thoughts came in a slow tangle; the meaning came and went like drifting dust particles crossing through a square of sunlight in the mall. I glanced up and then glanced away. It wasn't really what I'd call thinking.

████ helped me turn it into words, later. She guessed the endpoint before I arrived there, but she let me take my time. As we spoke she grew solemn. All of this was caught up in the love, the forward-looking bloom of being part of another person, of choosing someone and being chosen; the two things happened alongside each other—cats on the same patch at different times—and they were incompatible. I thought about trees twining together: eventually, surely, one always hinders the other.

We made a small fire in the lost house's garden, in a hole someone else had used for a fire before us. Smoke got in my face and my clothes, and she told me about forest stories. *In fairy stories*, she said, *they're always wandering off into the forest, or living in the forest. I mean* The Forest, *with capital letters, the one which is everywhere. This whole place used to be covered in forest, didn't it? I asked. Before the ice.* She frowned. *I don't believe that. Not the whole place covered. Anyway, if the whole place was forest then how would people wander into it by mistake?* We both stood close to the fire and its light flashed on us. The world was black but if you stepped back you could see the outline of the mall against the sky, with one tree waving blackly from its roof, silhouette rising. *Where do they go in places which never had forests*, I wondered aloud. *The desert*, she said. *But it's not the same. You get different things in a desert story than a forest story. But we never had any deserts*, I said, *so we don't know*. I glanced in her direction and she was looking at the fire. *Did you ever see a pantomime*, she asked. *The audience shouts* behind you *and it's about a monster. But the monster they see isn't really the scary thing—it's the painted boards behind, the never-ending trees, the things hiding there, the crooked old ladies and the clearings . . . They know if you go in there you come out changed. Just like you did, little fox*, she teased me. *Don't run upstairs in a horror story*, I said. *Don't go in the woods in a folk tale. But you will*, she said, concluding the thought. *You have to*. I watched the fire with her, on its way now to embers, and wondered if maybe that was the real reason they cut it all down. The old forest, the jungle, which to me was only words.

The last time I saw her it was springtime. A slick of hardened snow still lined the gap between the house's north wall and the rise to the hedge, hidden from the sunlight which caught everything else. The river was high and the green shoots near the back door were almost yellow, and ▓▓▓▓▓ came to visit because it was cold at the mall and we knew no one else would be here. Mum was working and Holly was out more and more, over at the farm-share where her new friends had promised her a future. We lay down on my little bed in the middle room, both unsure; the blankets smelled of me, and the house was so cold that we tried to recover our clothes without moving. She looked around at my room. *What*, I said. Her skin was hot against my front; I was conscious of my body, a breathing thing with warm aches surprising the muscles. *I don't know*, she said, *I think it's not like a boy's room. You should see the schoolroom*, I said. *Maybe that would fit your expectations. What's a school room?* I felt her turn to me, the warmth of her back fading. I saw for a moment the shape of our separating bodies. I explained the schoolroom.

Holly came home after ▓▓▓▓ left, having had a hard day. She tried to argue with me, and I stood dishevelled in the kitchen, scavenging from the cupboards without facing her. She was unstoppable, fourteen herself now, impatient because she was more of an adult than me. Then she realised ▓▓▓▓▓ had been here. I never shared anything with her, she said. No stories, no girlfriends. I was barely a brother; I was selfish; I left her out. I tried to say I had my own things to worry about, I wasn't trying to hurt her, but it sounded hollow. I probably knew I was in the wrong.

Instead of apologising I looked at her coolly, amused like I would be if a vole tried to fight back when I pounced. *You're trying to turn this into a fight*, I said, removing myself from emotion. *You can keep trying or you can listen to what I'm saying*.

She slapped me, and I looked up and met her eyes in blank surprise. She was angry with the same fire which fuelled every fight Mum ever started. I backtracked. *You don't get it*, I said. *You're not the centre of my life. I can't make it true. You're not in charge*. She flared. *Don't talk to me like that*. Her voice was vicious so I laughed at it:

she shouldn't have said that. I could feel how my own anger would rise now in response to hers, irresistible once it began. *Don't talk to you like that?* I asked. *Holly you can't just make yourself the mother.* I was drunk on all of it. I decided this was how the world ought to be. I decided that the violence of life was the cost of its honesty. I couldn't contain my impulses because I didn't want to.

When she tried to slap me again I caught her by the forearm, and smacked her bottom in return. *Unacceptable*, I said, mimicking Dad as she once knew him half a decade ago. She writhed and wriggled under my arm, fighting to escape. My hand stung. *You. Do. Not. Talk. To. Me. Like. That.*

I felt her midriff twist, tightening into readiness, and then she bit me. I released my grip. I noticed two dishes standing near the sink, the window's light dappled by tree shadows, the shapes of wood in the rest of the dim space. She left a ring of marks in my hand and stormed away upstairs.

I left the house with no direction; I only wanted to be away from her, thinking as if she didn't exist. I thought if a storm came I would walk on, and let myself be cold and unhappy, and get sick and deserve it, and the idea fit well. I passed the lost mall and then slowly passed the village turning too, only realising a hundred yards later that I was farther east than I knew, and on unfamiliar ground. Somewhere behind me was the path to ██████'s parents' house.

I thought about Holly as a baby. I thought about wrestling with dad, about █████ and about forests and about work and about cold paths and birds' eyes and dead rabbits and long grass and the shouts of approaching men. I thought about my tail twitching. I wondered how I would make myself return to the house and face Holly. I didn't think about if anyone else would know, only about how it would feel meeting her eyes. I thought about how this feeling was nothing to do with childhood, and everything to do with two adults who would have to keep looking at each other for a long time to come. I wished I had known how easily a family comes apart.

I realised I could hear shouts now, here, approaching along the road, and not only in my mind. The road was lined by hedges shooting out into trees, reaching in above the height of traffic. It looked like dusk was closer than it was.

I hesitated and considered turning back, but they rounded the bend into view, half a dozen shapes swaggering. It was too late to avoid meeting; I told myself to walk on, ready to glide past with a blank face; they were arguing or joking with each other, hard to tell which, and nothing happened until I was two paces past them and I heard them stopping behind me.

Hey.

Hey, boy.

I turned, my face as neutral as I could make it. The man in the centre, who had called, spoke again. *You have some kind of problem?* I just shook my head, my brow creased in polite puzzlement. *I don't think so. Huh*, he answered, *then why did you barge my friend?*

Sometimes the mistake can't be unmade, and there's nothing left in the game but to play it out. *I'm sorry*, I said, *I didn't realise.*

Oh, he said, *so you're thick as well as rude.* Here he left a pause for me to answer, to protest or squirm, but I didn't, because I knew it would make no difference. I didn't see why I should beg for mercy if the plea would be rejected. I thought about the idiocy of the event. I thought about how I shouldn't even be here, and I realised that, even so, there was no element of chance in the way I chose what to be and how to live. If I had been five minutes later, yes; if I had taken the turning for the village, yes; if I had heard them before they saw me, yes; but also, if I had been the kind of person who works properly. If I had loved my sister better and cared about what she said. If I had chosen to be anything other than what I am. The trees leaned in and I noticed the flash of a knife. The men were jeering, smirking, talking themselves into action, but I didn't listen. I heard something else: the trees were singing.

It was the noise they always make in moving air, but for once I heard it. Not that I understood; it wasn't like that. It was the earth again, talking. I'd barely heard more than dim clues. What was it saying? Why had I not worked harder to catch the message? It seemed now like it was the only thing that mattered.

The knife flashed again. If I fought, they were going to kill me. If I grovelled, would they let me go? Maybe. Could I fly away? Maybe, once upon a time. Beneath the glamour of the knife and the smart talk I could see their flanks rolling with muscle, their teeth bared and their heads lowering as one organism. Dogs, I thought. They smell blood and remember, somewhere in their bones, that the frozen hills once belonged to them. A fox can outrun a dog, all day and all night, in a fair chase, but there was nowhere to run. The leader sneered. *Are you scared?*

I knew that I couldn't win, but the fact was irrelevant. *It's funny*, I answered him, talking as much to myself as to the pack. *I always think I'll feel scared, like real danger would leave me paralysed with fear. But now there's no getting out of it, and the fear's not coming. How about that? All I feel is alive.*

I jumped first, aiming my teeth like arrows at the leader's throat with a red scream on my black lips, and the others descended. You don't get to choose what you are; if you're lucky, though, you get to find out.

Was it too late? What's too late? If life is for finding your place in the world, how can it be too late, if you actually find it?

The picture of me resisted focus because I insisted the boy stood at the centre —the fox and the crow were peripheral fragments of inheritance to shrug off. I worked to ignore what the world was saying to me because I wanted to build my towers. But the voices I ignored knew best. Maybe someone stronger than me could have held the boy in his place, but for me the balancing act was unachievable: I had to choose one thing to be. Why did I love my own cleverness so much more than touch, dirt, smell, wings, here? It's hardly anyone else's fault I learned slowly.

There was, once, a violent rhythm; long before me, a rise and a fall of things, each born either to flourish or die and be slowly subsumed by the rest of it. I remember it now; it's inside me. Hands hold everything in check, new shoots trimmed back by machine, always on the edge of life, and never quite becoming. Hands hold things still despite knowing things can't be held still. They break the rhythm, insisting on a strange unnatural violence all their own. And, caught in mad dreams, they forget that things always end. Claws are wiser.

My sister is sitting beside me, willing me to wake up and show her I am here. She wants to apologise, but if I could go back for even one day, I wouldn't waste it now on words or on hands. ▮▮▮▮▮ was right, and I organise my life into two parts: the part before I saw her, before I knew anything, and the part that happened since. I wonder what she'll do.

Here knows. The lights are off. My paws are cold. Why can't I remember ▮▮▮▮'s name?

CODA

The Overstory
by Richard Powers

W.W. Norton & Company, 2019

READERS AND WRITERS of deindustrial science fiction will be nourished by *The Overstory* by Richard Powers. Although it is not a work of future fiction—it fast-forwards through the lives of characters beginning in the mid-twentieth century and winding up in today's world—it is an emotional incendiary that begs for us to write a myriad different sequels with our lives. By spending the first third of the book introducing us to his nine main characters one by one, Powers bends the rules of readerly attention like a bough covered in snow. Just when you feel topped off with character introductions he begins to weave his web. First two meet, then another and another. Although they do not all eventually meet, and not everyone lives to the end, they are all interconnected like the network of fungi that connects trees belowground. After all, that is the point. It is a book about trees as much as humans, and the connections that entwine us.

We meet an Iowan artist, a Chinese-American businesswoman, a Vietnam vet, a woman caring for her debilitated husband, and a shunned botanist, among others. But we also meet Mimas, a massive California redwood that is treesat by a few of the characters for a time. The humans are a cross-section of modern America, some more nature-sensitive than others at the start but all of whom experience a kind of conversion in their relationship to trees. Eventually five of them engage in various levels of civil disobedience—even ecoterrorism—on behalf of the trees. Along the way Powers educates us painlessly in an astonishing array of botanical facts. Trees communicate and experience something akin to emotions and memories. Forests are families and communities that include care and sacrifice: parent trees helping their children and elderly trees passing along their stores of nutrients before their final breath, all thanks to the fungal network that connects root to root for many square miles.

This is not only seamlessly woven into the narrative but particularly highlighted via the character of Patricia Westerford, the aforementioned shunned botanist. In the novel she has written a book, *The Secret Forest*, of which we get tantalizing excerpts. This drove me to find out if such a book actually exists. What I found was *The Hidden Life of Trees* by Peter Wohlleben with an afterword by a woman botanist, Dr. Suzanne Simard. Is she the real-life Dr. Patricia Westerford? Whatever the case, Powers (and Wohlleben) has caused me, already a silviphile, to deepen my love for our leafed neighbors and reconsider my complicity in consumer society's enslavement and abuse of these majestic creatures. It is this botanical epiphany that can fuel our literary imagination, causing us to storytell our way into a deindustrial future, a place where trees are people too.

The venerable Ursula K. Le Guin has a novella, "Vaster Than Empires and More Slow," that touches on this in a more traditional science fiction style. An interstellar survey team lands on World 4470 to discover it is a "pure phytosphere" (all plants, no animals) —and yet their most empathic crew member detects sentience. Later, another crew member postulates, "There are no individual plants, then, properly speaking. Even the pollen is part of the linkage, no doubt, a sort of windborne sentience, connecting overseas. . . . That all the biosphere of a planet should be one network of communica- tions, sensitive, irrational, immortal, isolated. . . ." Their arrival has generated a diffuse, planet-wide fear, but in the end the empath, Osden, finds a way to alleviate it.

So as it turns out, plant intelligence is not a fiction and we are the ones guilty of isolating ourselves from it. May our literature include all of nature's intelligences as we imagine the breakdown of the industrial world.

—Jon Andreas

Printed by Amazon Italia Logistica S.r.l.
Torrazza Piemonte (TO), Italy

11727483R00062